To Love & Cherish

To Love & Cherish

To Love & Cherish

Colleen Reece

THORNDIKE
CHIVERS

This Large Print edition is published by Thorndike Press®, Waterville, Maine USA and by BBC Audiobooks, Ltd, Bath, England.

Published in 2005 in the U.S. by arrangement with Colleen L. Reece.

Published in 2005 in the U.K. by arrangement with the author.

U.S. Hardcover 0-7862-7275-9 (Candlelight)
U.K. Hardcover 1-4056-3295-X (Chivers Large Print)

The text of this Large Print edition is unabridged.
Other aspects of the book may vary from the original edition.

Set in 16 pt. Plantin by Ramona Watson.

Printed in the United States on permanent paper.

British Library Cataloguing-in-Publication Data available

Library of Congress Cataloging-in-Publication Data

Reece, Colleen L.
    To love and cherish / by Colleen Reece.
       p. cm. — (Thorndike Press large print Candlelight)
    ISBN 0-7862-7275-9 (lg. print : hc : alk. paper)
    1. Physicians — Fiction.   2. Mountain life — Fiction.
3. North Carolina — Fiction.   4. Trials (Murder) —
Fiction.   5. Distilling, Illicit — Fiction.   6. False testimony
— Fiction.   7. Forgiveness — Fiction.   8. Large type
books.   I. Title.   II. Thorndike Press large print
Candlelight series.
    PS3568.E3646T6 2005
    813'.54—dc22   2004025062

1

Dr. Edward Lucas paused on the top step of the vine-covered mansion, eyes gleaming in the early twilight. "Thanks, Sam," he called back to the carriage driver. "Don't wait. You know Miss Felicia."

He caught the wide, white grin that split Sam's black face as Sam chuckled. "Yassir, I does."

A sympathetic reflection tilted Dr. Luke's own lips in an upward curve. It lingered as he pulled the old-fashioned bell, then turned back to feast his eyes on the glorious world that surrounded him. Had any man ever lived in a more beautiful place than Charlotte in the mid-1800s? The door swung open.

"Miss Felicia's in the lib'ry, Doctor." The well-trained servant started down the hall.

"Don't bother to announce me. I'll go on in."

"But she's —" The servant's protest was lost in Dr. Luke's rapid progress down the hall. The library door was ajar, the room dimly lighted.

Dr. Luke paused, the smile on his lips deepening. How glad he was to be early! There would be time to tell Felicia his news before dinner. For a moment her image swam in his brain: golden-haired, haughty, beautiful beyond belief — and his. Yet even Felicia must not interfere with this perfect moment. At thirty years of age he had been selected for the post of head surgeon at the hospital he'd longed to serve ever since his scrimping, saving days in medical school.

It was worth it — every sleepless night, the tears he had privately shed over patients he lost — he jerked himself back to the present, humility flooding through him. His friends had nicknamed him Dr. Luke because of his devotion to duty. Luke, beloved physician. His heart swelled. Tomorrow night at the hospital ball his appointment would be announced. Would Felicia consent to a second announcement? What better place for their engagement to be made public? The cream of society would be gathered at the ball.

His smile faded. Felicia had been strange lately, almost distant. When he pressed her for a decision her brilliant smile had gone cold. "You know I'm going to marry you. I just don't want it announced yet."

Had she been waiting to see if he got the coveted post? He dismissed the thought as unworthy, but it refused to flee. There were several other leading North Carolinians eager for her favor. Many were more important than Edward Lucas. His blue eyes chilled. He would insist on her permission to announce their engagement at the ball before he told her of his selection as chief surgeon.

The heavy door opened noiselessly. In the flaring light from the huge stone fireplace a dark figure was etched. Before Dr. Luke's eyes it divided. Felicia? In the arms of another man? Impossible! He opened his mouth to cry out in protest, but was silenced by the impassioned voice of the other man. The hoarse, rapid breathing hit Dr. Luke with the force of a speeding ball.

"Felicia, how are we going to tell Dr. Luke?"

Dr. Luke fought the black cloud threatening to envelop him. "It won't be necessary. Dr. Luke already knows." He deliberately chose a splinter from the fireplace and lighted the large lamp nearby.

"Darling!" Felicia's face was a study in emotion as she ran to him, lips pouting, arms outstretched. "You mustn't — you don't think —"

He caught her before she propelled herself into his arms. "I am not sure just what I think, my dear." Was this his calm voice, giving no hint of his churning inside? "It is hardly the custom to find your fiancee in the arms of your best friend." He bowed to the white-faced man opposite, "Good evening, Jeffrey."

There was a strangled sound from his rival as Jeffrey turned toward him. "Edward —"

"My *friends* call me Dr. Luke."

"I know." The ashen lips seemed unable to form words. "I must talk with you alone."

"Why?" The hand that could be so rocklike in surgery trembled, but Jeffrey and Felicia did not see. "If you could take her from me so easily, perhaps she never was really mine." Every beat of his heart denied his statement.

Felicia smiled at one, then the other. "I'll just leave you to explain, Jeffrey." She lightly caressed Dr. Luke's rigid arm as she gathered her wide skirts and swept toward the door, then froze in place. "Who are you, and what do you want?"

Her icy demand didn't dent the stern

face of a uniformed officer, who stepped into the library followed by two others. "Sorry, miss. I have some questions for these gentlemen."

"Flyn?" Dr. Luke was familiar with the sheriff from his work in the hospital. "What's the trouble?"

"I've got orders to bring you in for questioning."

Dr. Luke could see mingled doubt and pity in the reddish-brown eyes under hanging eyebrows. "Question me?"

"Can you prove where you were last night?"

"I stayed at the hospital until midnight then went straight home."

Friendship vanished as Flyn slowly drew a battered medical bag from behind him. "This was found by the body of an old man who'd been run down by a carriage. Is it yours? Your name's in it."

Dr. Luke stared at the bag. "Yes, it's mine, but —"

A crash behind him cut off his explanation. He whirled toward the fireplace. In the split second before Jeffrey bent to pick up the shattered pieces of the vase he'd knocked over, Dr. Luke saw his eyes. Never had he seen such naked agony — and something else. Pleading? But why? In

11

spite of himself he responded. He slowly turned back to Flyn. "I can't explain why it was where you say."

"Come on. No sense wasting any more time." The sheriff coughed and motioned Dr. Luke out.

It had to be some kind of nightmare. Dr. Luke would never forget the scene: the burly officers; himself, being led past Felicia; Jeffrey —

"I'm coming with you."

"No need for that, Dr. Carr."

"I'm coming." The set jaw brooked no further argument. Yet through the questioning Jeffrey said nothing. It wasn't until Dr. Luke had been given the details of the incident and locked in a small cell that Jeffrey turned in answer to Dr. Luke's quiet question, "All right, Jeffrey. What's it all about?"

Jeffrey's haggard face did not lighten. "Thanks for not telling them you loaned me your bag last night. I didn't know anything would come of it!" He groaned. "I can't believe what I've done."

Dr. Luke could feel his face turn to granite. "Just tell me what you *have* done. I find you making love to Felicia. The law comes in and charges me with running down an old man, giving medical help, and

12

then leaving him to die after conveniently forgetting my bag. Suppose you tell me what I am guilty of — and why you kept your mouth shut out there."

"I had to." Jeffrey's face was gray with pain. His eyes unflinchingly met Dr. Luke's. "I'm not quite the rotter you believe. It's true I love Felicia. I always have."

"We'll leave her out of it until later."

Jeffrey shivered at the finality in the words. "I was dog tired. You know how it is after too many hours at the hospital. Yet I'd promised to stop by and see Mr. Carpenter no matter how late it was."

"What I don't know is how you got into such a mess," Dr. Luke said bitterly, "and got me into it as well."

"I left the hospital, fighting sleep. I was driving faster than I should have been, but the streets were deserted, or so I thought. I had Brown Billy almost at a gallop when I got to where Main Street crosses Second. By the time I saw the huddled figure in the street, it was too late. Brown Billy reared — tried to jump — but the carriage was too heavy." Jeffrey shuddered and passed one hand over his eyes. "I jumped out, ran back, automatically grabbing your bag. There was nothing I could do."

"You say he was there *before* you hit him?"

"Yes, and I believe he was already dead."

Dr. Luke sank talonlike fingers into Jeffrey's shoulders. "Then why did you run?"

Jeffrey swallowed hard. "I had no choice." The pleading that had been in his face earlier returned. "I've been warned by the hospital that any more notoriety would be grounds for dismissal." His laugh was harsh. "Funny, the one time I wasn't to blame for racing through the streets, this happens! After the publicity about Dan Maginn and I racing and causing complaints by the worthy townspeople, the hospital board said 'no more.' The next complaint would be it."

"So you left my bag, knowing my record would bear the strain more than yours."

Hot color flowed into Jeffrey's pale cheeks. "Never! I panicked. I got Brown Billy back to the stable and cleaned him up. All the while I thought of what would happen if they found out." He threw his head up proudly. "It wasn't for myself."

Dr. Luke's snort brought another wave of color.

"You don't have to believe it, but it wasn't. My mother had a heart attack a

14

few months ago. The doctor said that with rest and no excitement she can be as good as ever. I took her to a specialist; wouldn't trust my own judgment. A sudden shock such as this could kill her."

"And now?"

Jeffrey sank to a chair. His arms reached out as if involuntarily reaching for strength. "Luke, believe me! I didn't know I left your bag. Since I did —" He could not finish.

"Since you did, you're asking me to take the blame."

Jeffrey went white to the lips, as if he'd been knifed. "I would do anything on earth to save my mother."

"Even to seeing a friend accused? Even to knowing the post of head surgeon is lost to me forever, no matter what the result of the inquest?"

"I have no choice."

The death knell sounded in Dr. Luke's heart. "Then neither do I."

"You'll do it?" Jeffrey gasped for breath. Something of Dr. Luke's attitude sent hope flaring in his eyes. "They'll discover the man was already dead. It will show up in the autopsy."

"How do you know that?" Dr. Luke demanded.

"I examined the body carefully. Outside of cuts and a broken arm, the carriage inflicted nothing to cause death."

"It still means my career."

"I know!" Regret and anguish mingled in the muffled cry. "Don't you know I'd give anything on earth for it to be different?" Jeffrey beat both fists against the chair in despair. "I can't do anything different, I can't. I may be dishonorable for what I have done about Felicia, but I would almost rather be dead than do this to you. It's my mother's life, not my own, that I'm asking for."

"If I agree, will you promise that never, so long as you live, will you do anything to make me regret it?"

"I will." Jeffrey's face convulsed, and he held out an unsteady hand. "I'll arrange bail and get you out of here."

It was on Dr. Luke's lips to say he wanted nothing from the man who was ruining him. He bit back the words. The savings he had accumulated toward his marriage was not sufficient for what lay ahead. "Good night, Jeffrey." The door slammed behind him, signifying the slamming of a far more important door. The post — gone. Everything he had struggled for was wiped out by the promise he had made. Memory of

Felicia's enchantment tore into him — only to be replaced by the way she'd looked when he left her home. Scales dropped from his eyes. His golden-haired goddess turned to brass.

For hours he paced the tiny cell. Surely it was a nightmare that would vanish with the coming of dawn. From childhood came memory of a verse learned at his mother's knee. "Greater love hath no man than this, that a man lay down his life for his friends." Wasn't that what he was doing? Laying down his very life's blood for Jeffrey?

"No!" He sprang to his feet. "What rot! Sacrifices like this went out of fashion years ago. I can't lose it all. I'll fight!"

He knew it was false as soon as he said it. Someone stood in his way. God? He laughed bitterly. The God he had known as a boy had allowed this to come on him!

No, not God, but a little woman with lined face who had come to see Jeffrey long ago, so proud of her son, the doctor. A little woman whose sunshiny face had seemed to Dr. Luke the kindest of any he'd seen since his own mother died. His lips were closed. He could not exchange his career for her life when he was dedicated to the very act of saving life.

Hatred of what fate had done to him gave way to contempt. If Jeffrey hadn't been weak and willful, there would have been no need for such a sacrifice. It was true the hospital board would never have forgiven him. Too many incidents in the past with Jeffrey in the wrong were stacked against his skill as a surgeon.

Dr. Luke felt color drain from his head and hastily sat down. Of all the ironies, the worst was that the chief surgeon's post would probably be given to Jeffrey! His former friend would have everything — and nothing. For even the position and Felicia would never take from Jeffrey the knowledge that it had all been gained at the expense of one who had loved him as a brother since they entered medical school together.

He awoke early to a thunderous knock. Sheriff Flyn, Jeffrey, and the head of the hospital board stood there. Dr. Luke groggily sat up.

"Come on. You're getting out of here." His superior leaned forward. "How could you do such a thing? No one would have questioned its being an accident if you hadn't run, Lucas."

Dr. Luke's heart sank. He had been tried and convicted in one word: "Lucas." Not

18

Dr. Luke, or even Edward. Just Lucas.

"The hospital cannot condone such action and publicity. What say you?"

Dr. Luke's steady gaze never wavered. He might be a fool, but he had charted his course. "Nothing."

"Nothing!" The apoplectic face before him threatened to burst. "You are accused of an unspeakable thing and say nothing?" The steely eyes grew shrewd. "Are you protecting someone?"

It was the supreme moment. The slightest suspicion could prove to have terrible consequences. "Is it reasonable any man would protect another at such a cost?" he lashed out. "Who but a fool would allow his work, his very life, to be sacrificed for anyone else? Tell me that!" In spite of his anguish he could not fail to note the torture in Jeffrey's eyes.

His ringing indictment must have been convincing. The hospital supervisor stiffened. "Then you will be expected to appear at the inquest."

"I will be there."

Jeffrey's chalky face was the last thing Dr. Luke saw when they dropped him off at the cottage that had been home for so long. A thrush raised its song from a nearby shrub, but he just scowled. The

19

world should be black instead of greening into spring.

He had barely bathed and changed when he had another visitor. He watched Felicia, black-swathed, glide into the cottage. She had never even deigned to drive past before.

A tear trickled from under her black veil. Had she donned it for anonymity?

"What are you going to do?"

He was instantly on guard. "About what?"

"About everything." She raised the veil with diamond-studded fingers. "I always loved Jeffrey, but you were so charming, and —"

"And you couldn't resist dangling another scalp from your belt."

She had the grace to color. "I just heard today they were going to name you head surgeon. If only you had told me sooner!"

"It would have made a difference?"

She leaned forward eagerly. "Of course. Edward —" Her fingers clasped in the small-child pose he had always found charming. "If I told everyone you were with me while the accident happened, you could still be head surgeon. We could get married right away. Even if you don't have as much money, you'll be respected." She fingered a button on his waistcoat. "Should I do that for you? It would prove I really love you. Kissing Jeffrey didn't mean anything."

The last of his ideals about her crashed. So help Jeffrey if Felicia ever discovered what had really happened out there in the street that night! He was filled with loathing. "You will never lie for me. I wouldn't marry you if you were the only woman on earth and I was the only man. Any feeling I ever had for you is deader than the old man. Get out, Felicia — and don't come back."

"You don't mean that." Her smile slanted her green eyes.

"If you say one more word, I'll tell everyone how you were secretly meeting another man. I'll be believed. Those in high places are always envied."

"You'll regret for the rest of your life what you did today."

"Don't hold your breath waiting."

She whirled to the closed carriage. "Sam, hurry up. If you ever tell anyone I was here, I'll order you whipped!"

A whirl of dust, a furtive, sympathetic glance from Sam, and they were gone. Yet her presence lingered. "And I worshiped her and would have married her!" Dr.

Luke heaved a shaking sigh. "I'm thankful I found out what she was —" He broke off. Thankful to whom — God? Never. God had allowed him to be betrayed. What part had he with God?

Dr. Luke asked himself the question over and over in the days that followed. The inquest was crowded. He was well known in Charlotte. The judge had to pound for order and threaten to clear the room.

Dr. Luke moved through it all as if in a trance. He never lied. He merely stated that when the body had been examined, the old man was found to have been already dead. The carriage-inflicted wounds were not the cause. When asked why he ran away instead of moving the old man he merely replied, "I have nothing to say."

Then, one blossom-laden spring day, it was over. Because of his former unimpeachable record he was admonished because of his reprehensible action and set free.

"There's something fishy about the whole thing," his superior told him sternly. "We can't keep you on here with all the publicity. Jeffrey Carr is being given the post we had planned for you to fill."

"He's a good surgeon." Dr. Luke held himself stiffly.

His superior shuffled papers. "I'll write you a recommendation. Get away from here. I have connections, and —"

"I am leaving medicine and surgery."

"What? Are you insane?" Papers on the desk leaped. "You don't blame yourself for an accident, do you?" He glared at Dr. Luke. "Besides, the man was *already dead*."

"I know." Dr. Luke stood. "I just don't want to practice medicine any longer." He would never tell anyone how the thought of medicine would bring nausea at remembrance of the whole mess.

"You can't walk out of your career like this. Get away for a while. Go somewhere you can think." Kindness beyond any he'd ever seen in the hospital director's stern countenance shone from the softened eyes. "Even a wounded dog needs to get away and lick his wounds. But that doesn't mean he doesn't come back to fight again. I don't believe you were ever in that carriage." He held up a hand to silence Dr. Luke. "I don't know or care who was or why you're throwing everything away on a quixotic gesture. I do know you are a born surgeon and God made you so."

"God!" Dr. Luke compressed his lips tightly. "Good-bye, sir."

As days and weeks passed, Dr. Luke

thought of what his superior had said. From a usually decisive person he seemed to have turned to a jellyfish. Old friends were not comfortable when they met him. He sold the cottage home. Sorting papers, he found an answer as to where he could go. He'd been too busy to sort them before, he supposed. He was amazed to discover his father had owned a small piece of land with a cabin in the western part of the state, almost to the Tennessee line. He got out a map and tried to locate it.

"No Stump Hollow." Throwing the map aside in disgust, he shoved away the idea of going there. Yet as more time passed and he grew more determined to break away, the idea of a cabin in the woods far from anyone he'd ever known became appealing. He'd have solitude and peace there. He could decide what to do with his future. With a shock he realized he hadn't really taken a holiday in over ten years! One day he went to the railroad station and inquired about Stump Hollow.

"Hmmm." The stationmaster put a grimy finger on his map. "Jest about can't get there from here."

Dr. Luke stifled a laugh. "Well, suppose a fellow had to get there?"

The man scratched his balding head. "I

reckon he'd have to take the train to Asheville. It'd be a toss-up from there. There's probably wagons goin' part way. Don't know about the last section."

Two weeks later Dr. Luke had to agree with the stationmaster; he didn't know about that last section, either. The wagon track had run out at Singing Waters, and the storekeeper there warned it was still a "fur piece to Stump Holler."

From his savings and sale of the cottage, Dr. Luke took money and acquired owner-ship of a lopeared mule named Beautiful, whose chief virtue was a cheerful disposi-tion. Although Dr. Luke learned early it took a hearty whack to get Beautiful going, the slow pace suited him. Away from Char-lotte, some of the deeply etched lines in his face began to smooth out. It was impos-sible to ride a mule and worry over any-thing else. He had been assured the rest of his "trappin's" would be sent on from Singing Waters when Jed Hathaway got over his "drunk" and could haul them in.

Dr. Luke took a deep breath of the sweet air, unconsciously pulling his coat closer. At nearly a mile high, the atmosphere made for chilly nights and mornings in spite of summer's approach. A tired smile lifted some of the somberness from his features. What would Stump Hollow hold for him? The storekeeper at Singing Waters had snootily lifted his nose and said, "Nobody ever heerd tell of anyone wantin' to live in Stump Holler! They're a quare bunch."

Maybe that was what he needed — a bunch as queer as himself. Outcast, alone, cursing himself for his quixotic gesture for the sake of an old woman he hardly knew, Dr. Luke traveled the trail to Stump Hollow and his new home.

2

"The storekeeper at Singing Waters was right." Dr. Luke ruefully rubbed his nearly numb legs. "It surely is a 'fur piece' to Stump Hollow." He gazed around him. He had been so caught with the freshness of this strange land he hadn't been watching the track they traveled.

"Hey, Beautiful." His mule cocked one long ear. "What did you do? Take some trail known only to you?"

The loud bray confirmed his suspicions. Perplexed, he halted the beast and considered. "Best thing to do is turn and get back to the main trail."

In vain he endeavored to get Beautiful turned. The faint trail they were on was narrow at that point, and the mule would not turn. After several futile attempts, Dr. Luke shrugged. "All right. Have it your way. We'll wait and turn in a wider spot like that one ahead." His eyes feasted on the sparkling stream and softly waving willows. What a place! If only his own cabin were to be in a little pocket between hills such as this!

"Small chance, with my luck," he muttered, then grinned at his sour tone. It didn't fit the peacefulness of his surroundings.

When they reached the wider spot, he slid to the ground and stiffly threw himself down to drink from the stream. The water was so cold it made his teeth ache and so pure he could see every glint of metal in the stones below its surface.

"Good!" He splashed more of the tingling water on his face, rejoicing in the shivers it produced against his skin. Beautiful had waded into the stream a few yards down and seemed to be enjoying it as much as Dr. Luke.

It wasn't until he drank deeply for the second time and raised his head that he saw it — a tiny shack nestled under a huge evergreen. A single curl of smoke spiraled toward the sky.

"Good! I can see if there's a shortcut back to the trail." Again he smiled wryly. Was he going to become a hermit so soon, talking to his mule for company? Leaving Beautiful with reins hanging as the former owner had instructed, Dr. Luke stepped from rock to rock across the creek and strode toward the cabin.

"Hello! Anyone home?"

There was no answer from the shack except another curl of smoke. On closer observation he saw it wasn't a shack after all, just an old shed half-hidden by the trees. If he hadn't been flat on his stomach by the creek he never would have seen it.

"Curious." He walked closer. What a strange contraption! A large vat, pipes, something dripping slowly into a dirty barrel. He couldn't resist sticking one finger in the mixture and smelling it. Whiskey!

"What're you doin' here?"

The husky voice spun him around on his heel. A slender boy clad in faded clothing and a hat that shadowed his face stood behind him.

It was ridiculous to feel embarrassed, but he felt his face flush. "I just saw the shack when I drank at the stream and thought I'd ask if there was a shortcut back to the main trail." He laughed, feeling even more foolish. "My mule seems to have been here before."

"He used to belong to —" The lad broke off, sheer terror in his big eyes. "You got t' get out of here before —"

Dr. Luke never knew what the "before" meant.

"Duck!" Surprisingly strong hands dragged him to one side, but not before he half turned. From the bushes a few rods away a long rifle barrel raised, steadied. In helpless fascination Dr. Luke watched, then felt a heavy blow to the left arm at the same moment he heard a loud *Spang!* and was jerked to the ground, hitting heavily on his right side. He felt his head slam hard, then all went black.

What seemed like a century later Dr. Luke heard voices, the husky one mingled with deeper tones. They were too far away for him to catch more than a few words: "Shouldn't have done it. . . . Deserves it, the sneak! . . . Git him outa here. . . . Dump him by the Holler."

Was it Beautiful's back he was being lifted onto? One almost-nerveless hand felt the saddle blanket and recognized it. Then blackness struck again.

The same blackness prevailed when he awoke, head throbbing but otherwise alert. He rubbed his eyes to be sure they were open. His heart leaped with fear. Had he gone blind?

From somewhere in the shadows the boy's voice spoke. "You'll be all right, mister."

"But I'm blind!"

Even through this panic Dr. Luke noted a rippling laugh, much like the little stream he had drunk from earlier that day. Or was it the day before?

"You aren't blind. We're in a cave."

A cave! Dr. Luke sank back against the blanket, conscious of new feelings. He was lying on a soft bed. Exploring fingers carefully touched his mattress, to discover it was made of boughs.

"I'll light a candle," the unseen boy promised. Moments passed, and Dr. Luke found himself straining his ears to hear. Was the boy an Indian, that he slipped so quietly about?

The candle stub flared. "See, it's all right."

"How did I get here?"

Something flickered in the deepset eyes. "I brought you."

"I heard someone say, the man who shot me, he was going to dump me by the hollow."

"He did. By Stump Holler. But I brought you here. You'd have bled to death if I'd let you be where he left you."

"But why would anyone want to shoot me?" In his anger Dr. Luke sat up, then fell back with a groan. Waves of pain shot through his left arm, leaving him light-headed.

"Mountain folk don't take kindly to furriners."

"So they shoot them?"

"Sometimes, if they're where they ain't supposed to be." The boy dropped to one knee, gathered a careful pile of twigs. He molded it into a cone and touched it with his candle.

"Do you know the man who shot me?"

The boy did not answer immediately. When he spoke again, it was on another subject. "I'm heatin' water to wash that arm." The brown hands went about their duties carefully. From a shadowy recess a blackened pot came forth, no stranger to fire. A water bottle filled the pot, and more wood lightened the cave. Only then did the boy come to Dr. Luke. "I stuffed rags in to stop the bleedin', but I've got to clean it now. You're goin' to have to help me get you out of that shirt."

It was a job. By the time the shirt was off and the wound exposed, beads of sweat stood on Dr. Luke's forehead. When the brown fingers pressed just above the gash, for a moment he thought he would be sick.

"The rifle ball is still in it."

Dr. Luke saw the boy catch his lower lip between his teeth.

"It's got to come out. Is there a doctor in

Stump Holler?" He substituted the mountain pronunciation for his new home.

"No doctor closer than Asheville."

"Asheville! I could be dead before getting there!" He bit back an exclamation of pain. "Boy, you'll have to help me get that bullet out."

"Me?" There was fear in the gasp as the boy dropped Dr. Luke's arm and stepped back. "Why, I ain't even got a knife! I've never done anything like this. I can't — oh, I can't!"

"You've got to." Dr. Luke's face was grim. "Either that man who shot me is in your family or you know who he is. Do you want him to hang for murdering an innocent stranger?"

Every trace of color fled the watching face. "But how can I — you can't expect me to —"

"Have you ever seen anyone die of gangrene?"

"No." The whisper came from colorless lips.

"The flesh rots away, and the victim dies." Dr. Luke was ruthless. In Charlotte he had almost begun to wonder whether life was worth living. Now he clung to it. He would not die this way, shot down by a common sneak when he was innocent of any wrong. "Do you want that to happen?"

Only a feeble shake of the boy's head interrupted him. "Then go to my saddlebags. There are instruments there —"

"You're a doctor?" Was that hope in the pale face?

"I was. You're going to have to help me. I can't do it myself, but I can tell you exactly what to do." Deep inside, thankfulness for that last-minute throwing in of his instruments warmed him, but there was no time for considering it now.

The boy was back in minutes, hands full.

"Bring me the smallest packet." He planned as he carefully unwrapped the shining instruments, selecting the ones he would need. "I'm going to tell you step by step what you have to do to get that bullet out."

"You don't mean you want me to *dig* in you!" Incredulity mingled with horror in the boy's face.

"That's just what I mean." He fixed a stern gaze on the boy. "Even if I scream, and I probably will, *don't stop probing.* You understand? The bullet has got to come out!"

"I understand." The pallid lips formed other words, indiscernible to Dr. Luke. Was the boy praying?

"You'll have to boil the scalpels. Also the probe. I don't have anything else to sterilize them."

"There's this." The lad drew out a small bottle of colorless liquid with dark brown settled to the bottom. "You could drink some for the pain."

"Whiskey?"

"Yes." The clear eyes met his. "I was going to wash out the hole in your arm with it."

"Good. Do it now. I can't drink it. I have to be alert."

There was a slight tremble in the brown fingers as they poured the liquid fire over the bloody area. Dr. Luke frowned. "Your hands will have to be steadier than that to operate. Take a drink of that whiskey."

He wasn't prepared for the fire that flared in the other's face. "Never!"

"You need it."

"I'd sooner die than drink that stuff!"

He couldn't force the issue. "All right, but you're going to need something to do this." He gazed at the arm now exposed, blood seeping out. He shuddered as the boy removed the last of the rags. Probably filthy. The whiskey would have its work cut out for it, killing germs that could have come from those rags.

"God will help me do it." Something in the boy's pearly face stilled Dr. Luke's involuntary protest. If the boy believed in God, let him use his belief to get through the ordeal ahead.

And it was an ordeal. The ball was lodged in the fleshiest part. Once he determined exactly where it was, Dr. Luke grunted. At least it wasn't shattering a bone. But why hadn't it gone clear through? He wondered aloud.

"When I jerked you down it hit your pocket and glanced." The boy felt in his shirt pocket and withdrew a small object.

"Ironic!" Dr. Luke stared at the small metal box. In it were precious matches. He hadn't known if the handy invention would have reached Stump Hollow yet.

"So small, to save your life." For the first time a faint smile crossed the boy's face. "God must've been protecting you."

"Don't talk to me about God!"

The boy was silenced.

Dr. Luke was sorry for shouting. This nightmare had to be incredibly horrible to the young boy. "I'm sorry. Let's get on with the operation."

By the time the ball was out and the wound rewashed with whiskey, Dr. Luke was even whiter than the temporary surgeon. He smiled weakly. "Boy, you've saved my life. There's a saying that if someone saves your life, you belong to that person. If I can ever do anything for you —" The effort was too great. He sank back on the boughs. This time his sleep was the sleep of exhaustion. He only roused when the boy forced him to sit up slightly and take hot broth. He neither knew nor cared how the broth had been made. All he wanted to do was rest.

Sometime in the void that followed he roused enough to see the boy asleep on the floor next to him. The dying fire shone on a lock of curly brown hair that had escaped through a hole in the old hat.

Admiration filled him. The mountain boy had passed the hardest test possible with banners flying. What other lad of his acquaintance would have done it?

When he dropped off to sleep again, it was with one hand touching the little brown hand inert between them.

In spite of the whiskey-bath, the wound infected. Dr. Luke knew when it started. He had seen so many similar cases! The fever, rising until delirium, subsiding — one hoped — once the infection was burned out. For days he lay uncaring, yet conscious of passing time. Strange fancies filled him. If he died here, only the boy would know — and the marksman. No one in Charlotte had any idea of where he was.

He couldn't die. There was something he had to do first. It plagued his brain, refused to let him give up completely. He owed a debt to someone, a debt that must be paid. Why couldn't he remember? Incoherent ramblings rang in his ears. His own? Why, why couldn't he forget it and sink into oblivion?

Occasional glimpses of the boy brought him back to the edge of reality. If he died, would the boy be blamed? He couldn't let that happen. Were those the fires of hell that raged within him, or just fever? The boy talked to God. Was God there?

Even as the inquest in Charlotte had ended, now the fever and infection ebbed away at the inexpert but insistent nursing of the boy. Dr. Luke awoke tired but rational. He recognized the cave where he'd been brought and wondered again how such a slim youth could have managed his own bulk.

"Boy?" This whisper didn't get beyond his own lips.

"Boy." This time he succeeded in rousing the pale-faced boy who slept huddled against the opposite wall of the cave.

Sleep-filled eyes suddenly came alive. "Why, you're purely better!"

"Yes." It was all he could get out.

More broth. Soft sweet potatoes baked in the coals. A bit of bread. Gradually Dr. Luke's shrunken stomach learned to hold food again. The jagged scar no longer oozed. He was getting well.

A few days later Dr. Luke leaned on the willing shoulder of his rescuer and hobbled to the mouth of the cave. Never had he seen anything more welcome than the shining stream, swaying willows, and wild-flowers. How could he ever have thought life was no longer worth living? What were Felicia and Jeffrey and their treachery by comparison to this beautiful world?

"Beautiful."

The boy's mouth widened in a smile. "He's been perfectly happy this past week. Been croppin' grass till he was full, then rollin' in it."

The soft accent didn't keep him from shock. "A week? I've been here a week?"

"Yes." A cloud formed in the sunshine of the boy's face. "Mister, you said you owed me —"

Ah, this was it. What he'd tried to remember. "Anything."

"Would you go on to Stump Holler as if

you were just commin' in from Singin' Waters? No one's expectin' you, are they?"

"No, but I don't see —" An inkling of the reason for the request reached him. "You mean don't say anything about being shot? Who are you protecting?"

"It don't matter. Will you do it?"

"And leave the miserable skunk to shoot some other innocent man? Never!" He could feel the shoulders droop beneath his weight as if suddenly tired. The next moment his own shoulders slumped. "Boy, if that's your price, I've got it." The slight form supporting him went rigid.

"You mean you'll do like I ask?"

"Yes, but why? Why do you want it unknown? Don't you want people to know you saved my life?"

"No one must ever know that!" The boy clung to him in terror. "If anyone in Stump Holler knows I was here with you — you'd be killed!"

Dr. Luke's surprise stood him upright, leaning against the cave entrance for support, releasing the boy. "Why on earth? You can't mean it!"

Some tragedy lurked in the haunted eyes. He hadn't been able to see them in the cave. Now they stood out in the boy's white face — glowing violet with little brown specks, like a wood violet he had once seen.

With a laugh the boy obviously had changed from a sob, he raised one hand, threw aside the covering hat.

Dr. Luke reeled. The boy was no boy, not with a glorious crown of hair like that! His rescuer, the companion who had stayed with him day and night, who saved his life, nursed him, and now implored for his silence stood unashamed before him.

A woman. No, a girl, not yet into womanhood.

"But you, but I —" He could not go on.

"If you'd known I was a girl, would you've let me stay?" Her honest eyes met his.

"No." He had to ask the question. "Why did you?"

Her expressive eyes shadowed. "I know the woods. I never pass a hurt critter. God'd not have me pass you by."

He found himself staring. Was she so innocent, so unconscious of her own wild beauty she did not know all it could have meant if he'd been less ill or a different kind of man? "You risked your reputation — your good name for me."

Her voice was melodious, strangely free of bitterness. "I've no good name, as you'll hear soon enough." She whistled a strange note and was rewarded with Beautiful's slow ambling to where they stood. "You're able to ride now. Go on to Stump Holler, but say nothin' of what happened." She packed his instruments carefully and helped him mount in the stricken silence he could not seem to break.

"Good-bye, mister." She smiled faintly with her mouth but not her eyes. "Trail's that way." She pointed through leafy green.

He finally found his tongue. "Wait! Will I see you again? Do you live near? I don't even know your name."

"My name's Cherish." The willows closed behind her.

Dr. Luke sat stupefied. "Come back. Cherish, come back!"

Only the waving branches nodded a reply. The girl Cherish had gone, leaving Dr. Luke astride a mule already starting down the overgrown trail to Stump Hollow. It wasn't until a low branch threatened to unseat him that Dr. Luke's whirling senses steadied and acknowledged what was insistently pounding for recognition: Cherish was lame. He closed his eyes. Was it from his leaning on her, his weight resting on her slight build?

No. Even in his delirium it must have

registered. She walked with one foot drag-ging.

I have no good name as you'll hear — Her voice echoed in the little glade along the trail. Her tragic eyes etched themselves against a mighty tree. What was her secret, this strange girl who called on God, pro-tected a killer, and cared for a stranger? Above all, why was he so impatient to get to Stump Hollow? Why not rein in Beau-tiful, turn around, and flee this part of the Great Smokies?

Instead Dr. Edward Lucas set his jaw, whacked Beautiful to a faster pace, and set his face forward to whatever lay ahead.

3

"What've I done?" Cherish sank to the needlecovered ground a few hundred yards from where she'd left the stranger. "I don't know his name. Who're Jeffrey and Felicia, and what'd they do to him?" Her slight form quivered. "If Jed finds out I fetched the stranger to the cave and took care of him —" She shuddered.

The sleepless nights had taken a toll her patient couldn't know. Now Cherish buried her face in her hands and pillowed her head on a clump of grass. The sun's rays fell on the bowed head, and she slept.

When Cherish awoke it was nearly dark. Reluctantly she dragged herself up and took the trail leading to a shack perched tipsily on the side of the mountain. Her lame foot dragged more than usual. What would her father say, after her being gone all those days? For the very first time she almost hoped he would be drunk. The next moment her face blanched. No, not that! She still had bruises on one shoulder from his last drunk. When her father was sober he tolerated her; when drunk — she shuddered. All the devils in the world couldn't be worse than Jed when he was drinking. Yet his still in the woods was never silent. Always it dripped, dripped, dripped, bringing damnation to Jed and his small circle of cronies that habited it.

"If I'd anywhere else to go, I'd never go back to him!" Cherish told herself, but her shoulders slumped as they had when the stranger leaned on her. She had been through it a dozen times. She had no choice but to stay with Jed. People of Stump Holler had nothing to do with her. It didn't even bother her anymore. They thought because her leg was crooked, she was cursed of God. They also thought she was "teched" in the head because she preferred the company of the animals in the forest to their half-hidden stares when she had to go to the store.

Involuntarily, her fingers sought the hard lump inside her worn shirt. She had managed to keep it from Jed. It was the only thing left of her mother's. Her calloused hands stroked the cover. If only she could read it! Once she timidly suggested to Jed that she'd like to go to the tiny school Stump Holler finally got for the children.

She wouldn't soon forget his answer.

"You!" He spat in the dirt, narrowly missing her bare feet. "The school's fer young'ns, not sich as you!" He spat again, dirty tobacco juice staining the ground. "You got enuf to do keepin' this place, hear?"

She never asked again. Yet deep inside was a dream. Someday she was going to learn to read. If she could have stayed with Granny — Cherish shook her head. It didn't pay to think of what could have been.

The shack looked dingier than ever. The tiny garden she had worked so hard to make was the only cheerful spot near. She was longing for the greens in that garden. Winter vegetables and hog fat got tiresome.

Slowly she pushed open the door.

It was as she feared. Her father was drunk again, lying in a stupor. Cherish sighed with relief. At least he wouldn't be asking where she'd been. With an unaccustomed curiosity she left the door open so the final bit of daylight would shine in the dark cabin, and stepped to her father's side. The glance she gave him turned to consideration. How different was the haggard, bearded unkempt man from the stranger, even though he also had had a growth of beard.

Why had her mother ever married him? What had she seen in the man now prone on the bed, blankets half off the straw tick? Cherish looked closer. Nothing could have unriveted her gaze. Somehow she had to know — was there anything good at all about her father?

Harsh lines furrowed the bearded cheeks from brow to chin. He couldn't be over forty, but he looked like an old man.

Cherish turned away, a lump in her throat, not because of love for her father, but because she had never been given a father to love. "Why couldn't you have been like — like him?" she whispered, thinking of the stranger. "Why'd you up and turn on me?"

Only a low moan answered her, and in panic she turned to flee. If she roused Jed now, it would mean anger, blows, more hatred.

Leaving the door propped open in case he called for her, Cherish quietly took a blanket from the other bed and slipped out. She would sleep under the stars as she did so often. Somewhere past them was her mother — and God.

By the time Dr. Luke reached the cluster of buildings that must be Stump Holler it was nearly dark. His left arm ached, and he had never been so tired in his life.

A tiny twinkle of light in an uncurtained window caught his attention, and he guided Beautiful toward it. Stiffly he dismounted and walked toward the door, but was stopped by a low growl. From the growing darkness a long shape detached itself from the porch and gathered for a spring.

"Down!" A voice from the square of yellow light made by someone throwing open the door halted the dog, but didn't stop it from growling again. "Who're you and what d' you want?"

Dr. Luke was getting tired of his welcome to Stump Hollow. First someone shot at him, then a dog almost tore him apart, if the growl was any evidence, now a wizened old man peered from the doorway.

"My name's Lucas. May I come in?"

The door was grudgingly opened a little wider. "C'mon."

Dr. Luke was almost blinded by the lamp the old man deliberately held up as he entered.

"Reckon yore peaceable."

Suddenly the humor of the whole thing got the better of Dr. Luke. He had come to Stump Hollow looking for a different world. He had found it!

"Mind getting the light out of my eyes now that you've decided I'm peaceable?"

The old man cackled and set the lamp on a table. For the first time Dr. Luke could get a glimpse of his reluctant host. The most arresting feature was the bright blue eyes peering from the sun-stained face. Keen intelligence, even humor, shone from them. Dr. Luke's gaze swept the cabin. Dirt floor. Chinked walls. Faded calico curtains. But everything was clean. He breathed a sigh of relief. He hadn't known what to expect, but at least the place was clean. His spirits lifted.

"Name's Lucas, aye? I'm Uncle Billy." The old man smiled.

"Do you always greet strangers like you did me?" Dr. Luke wished he had held his tongue. Some of the humor faded from the watching blue eyes.

"Son, last time Hound howled like that I lost six of my best chickens to some low-lived thief!" Dr. Luke was speechless, but Uncle Billy went on. "You don't look like no chicken thief, but a body cain't be too careful." His ill-fitting teeth clattered as he chuckled. "So how about declarin' yourself?"

Something of respect for this shrewd old man glimmered in Dr. Luke, coloring his

49

reply. "As I said, my name's Edward Lucas. They call me — Luke." He had almost said "Dr. Luke." "There's a piece of land with a cabin somewhere up here that's mine now my father's dead. I'm going to find it and live there."

Uncle Billy's face was bright with interest. "So! You aim to live on the old Lucas patch."

"You know it?"

The old man's laugh was short. "Who don't?" His eyes bored into Dr. Luke. "The house ain't much, but it's in the purtiest country around here."

Like a ray of hope his words lifted Dr. Luke's flagging spirits. "Can you tell me how to get there? How far is it?"

"Sho, you cain't go tonight." Uncle Billy cast him a measuring glance. "You kin sleep in the loft if you want. Tomorrer I'll show you."

Dr. Luke finally found his voice. "You mean, stay here with you?"

"Fer the bright boy you 'pear to be, you ain't catchin' on. That's what I said." The keen blue eyes raked the visitor. "You're tired, been hurt — bloodstains on your shirt. I'm a purty good hand at doctorin'."

Dr. Luke managed to hold back his automatic response and substituted. "Fell on

50

a sharp branch." He couldn't betray the boy — no, the girl whose name was Cherish.

"Whatever you say." But Dr. Luke knew he hadn't fooled Uncle Billy when the old man added, "Branches up here kin be mighty sharp. So kin bullets." He deliberately pointed to the loft. "If I cain't help you, you can bed down up there."

"Thanks."

But as Dr. Luke mounted the steep steps crudely fashioned to get to the loft he heard Uncle Billy's parting remark, "You ain't no chicken thief, then how come you got — hurt?"

Dr. Luke wisely ignored him and called, "Good night." He hadn't fooled the old man one minute. Uncle Billy knew he'd been shot. What should he do? If he refused to discuss it, would Uncle Billy gossip until word got around? What if he told the old man the truth, asked him to keep quiet about it? He'd bet Uncle Billy would never break a promise. Could he tell about being shot without involving Cherish?

He was still debating it when he fell asleep. It wasn't until Uncle Billy beat on a pan and he sat up with a start that Dr. Luke realized he still hadn't solved his problem.

"Come and get it." Uncle Billy needed to issue no second invitation. The smell of frying ham and boiled coffee lured Dr. Lucas to the table in a hurry. He reached for his fork, but was abashed when the old man dropped his head. "Lord, for what we are about to eat, we give thanks. Amen."

Dr. Luke could feel embarrassment flush his face. Who would have thought this old man would say a blessing? To cover his feelings he blurted out, "Uncle Billy, if I tell you something will you keep it to yourself?"

Uncle Billy didn't even look surprised. "Shore. Never was much of a hand to run off at the mouth."

Forgetting even the appealing breakfast before him, Dr. Luke weighed his words carefully, sorting each one. "I got off the main trail on the way here. Must have been dreaming, and Beautiful —" He broke off, remorse in his face. "I didn't take care of my mule last night."

"Did it fer you. Go on."

The terseness helped. "When I drank from a stream I saw a shack. Thought I'd get directions. I found a barrel and pipes — whiskey."

"Jed Hathaway's still. Makes his own moonshine."

Dr. Luke's fork clattered to the table. "A still!"

"Cheaper than buyin' it." Uncle Billy's loquaciousness seemed to have undergone an eclipse. "Go on."

Dr. Luke wrinkled his forehead. "Jed Hathaway? I've heard that name. Oh, the storekeeper at Singing Waters said someone named Jed Hathaway would haul in my stuff when he got over his drunk."

"Same Jed." Uncle Billy put in drily. "Good packer when he ain't drinkin'."

"Anyway" — Dr. Luke hastily skipped a bit — "I saw a rifle barrel rise. Next thing I knew I woke up with a bullet in me, but I wasn't by the shack anymore."

"Hmmm. See who shot you?"

"No."

"How'd you git here? Is the ball still in you?"

"I managed to get it." It sounded weak even to Dr. Luke, and he added the one thing he had vowed not to disclose to anyone in Stump Hollow. "I was a doctor; had my instruments on Beautiful."

"So you come to with a bullet in you, managed to get it out one-handed, waited till you felt better, then come here."

Dr. Luke felt his color rise again but

steadfastly refused to rise to the bait. "Something like that."

Uncle Billy leaned back and surveyed him with wise eyes. "Jed Hathaway's not known for shootin' people then patchin' 'em up." He broke off, then innocently asked, "See anythin' of Jed's daughter?"

"Daughter!" The surprise in Dr. Luke's face was real. "He has a daughter?"

"Shore. He ain't much of a father, but he's got a daughter." Uncle Billy's sharp eyes softened. "She ain't had much of a life, the way I hear tell."

"Oh?" It took every bit of willpower Dr. Luke had to keep his voice politely interested without sounding eager.

"Yep. Jed come here when the kid was maybe four or five or six. Nobody knows how old she is. Nobody even knew he had a kid for a long time, then someone saw her runnin' through the woods on that lame leg of hers —"

"Lame leg!"

He knew it was a mistake as soon as he repeated the words, but Uncle Billy gave no sign to indicate unusual interest.

"Folks around these parts won't have anythin' to do with her. First there's that quare name — Cherish. Someone asked her if her name wasn't Charity, like Jed had told everyone. The little old thing just raised up and said her ma named her Cherish and that was what she aimed to be called.

"Then there was Jed. I asked him about the gal, and he swore terrible. Said she was worse'n a murderer. Her ma died when she was borned, jest after namin' her. There was a curse on the baby, that's how come she's lame and walks with a crooked foot."

"What rot!" Dr. Luke shoved back his chair and glared at Uncle Billy. "You don't believe such stuff, do you?"

"I didn't say I did. But most folks 'round here do. That's how come they won't have nothin' to do with the gal. Besides, she kin tame the animals. Even old Hound sidles up alongside her fer a pat if she goes by. Folks think she'll put a spell on them if they cross her, so they jest leave her be."

Uncle Billy chuckled, chewed another mouthful, and swallowed. " 'Pears you're mighty interested, seein' as how you're a stranger and all." If he noticed Dr. Luke's sudden silence he blandly ignored it. "She's got a hand with sick things. If ever I had a bullet in me, I'd call fer her. Don't know if she's ever dug one out, but I bet she could do it."

A slow smile crept over Dr. Luke's face.

He could feel it even from inside. "I'll bet she could."

Uncle Billy seemed to have lost interest in the subject. "Eat up, now. We'll git out to the old Lucas place before dinnertime."

"Uncle Billy," he had to ask, "how old would this Cherish Hathaway be now?"

"Who knows? Like I said, she was four or five or six when she came. That's been twelve, no, fourteen year ago. I remember it 'cause it was the worst winter we ever had. Pitiful little thing, ragged clothes, bare feet. At that, it's the best she's ever had. Jed's too stingy to buy her dresses. She wears his old clothes when he's ready to throw 'em away."

Dr. Luke was calculating rapidly. "Then she must be between eighteen and twenty now!" He was shocked. That slight, boyish figure — how could she be that old? "Did you ever hear any more about her, before she came?"

"Word has it she lived with her granny till the old woman died. I reckon Jed didn't know what else to do with her but fetch her with him. She's been keepin' house fer him ever since she got old enough." The corners of his mouth turned down. "Jed Hathaway's so mealy-mouth no one'd ever know anythin' if they didn't see it, like the bruises on the gal."

Fresh horror hit Dr. Luke. "Bruises! You mean — ?"

"Yep. I seen 'em myself, one time I come on her fishin' with her sleeves rolled up."

"Why didn't you do something about it?"

"He's her paw."

The anger inside Dr. Luke spurted. "So what? She should be taken away, put somewhere he can't get to her! The law would —"

"Ain't got no law here." Uncle Billy must have heard his sharp intake of breath. "Don't have to like it, but that's how it is. 'Sides, where'd she go if she was away from Jed? Nobody around here'd have her, 'cept maybe me, and how'd I take care of a gal?"

Dr. Luke's rage threw aside his caution. "Then this is the kind of people who live up here! Willing to let an innocent person suffer because it's 'the way it is.' " His voice was an exact imitation of Uncle Billy.

"You ain't got no scoundrels back where you come from? No folks who'd do you dirt?"

Dr. Luke's anger died. Jeffrey's and Felicia's faces rose in front of him. "Yes, Uncle Billy. We've got them where I come from."

The old man's eyes turned kind. "Son, folks is folks, no matter where you live. They're good and they're bad, and sometimes both. Don't make no never mind if they live in cities or in Stump Holler, folks is always goin' to be the same."

"But can't anything be done for the girl?"

Uncle Billy sat back and slowly put down his fork. "If sometime someone could court and marry Cherish, she'd be took care of. Would have to be a stranger. Jed's already run off the only fella what had the gumption to go callin'." He crossed to the wooden peg and took down his patched coat, caught up his rifle. "Let's go. Maybe we kin pot a squirrel for supper."

It wasn't more than a half mile from Uncle Billy's to what he had dubbed "the purtiest country around here." He had also been accurate about the cabin. Never had Dr. Luke seen such squalor. Someone had broken the latch, and the door stood gaping open. A stench of stale whiskey, animal droppings, and musty, unused surroundings forced them back.

"It kin be cleaned." Uncle Billy seemed to divine his thoughts. "Look out there."

Dr. Luke followed the indicating hand.

What a contrast! Gently sloping hillsides rose to higher mountains. A warm breeze blew in pine-scented air. There wasn't a sound for miles except the breathing of the two men, Beautiful, and Hound. One rock outcropping lorded it over the valley below, the "pocket" containing Stump Hollow and mercifully hiding it from view.

"If it was me," Uncle Billy said casually, "I'd git me some cleanin' rags and set to work." He surveyed the cabin. "Built solid. Won't take much mendin' to have a mighty fine place."

"I can't imagine it ever being clean enough to live in," Dr. Luke confessed.

"Git a broom and hot water and strong lye soap. But not today," the old man told him. "That arm ain't up to hard work yet." He gazed down at Stump Hollow. "Course if a man had a bit of money, he could git someone to clean fer him — someone like Cherish Hathaway, mayhap."

"You old schemer!" Dr. Luke laughed out loud and was pleased to see Uncle Billy laugh back. "Mayhap I'll do just that."

"Better let me tend to it. Don't know how Jed'd like his gal workin' fer a single doctor."

"I don't want folks here to know I'm a doctor."

"Why not? You ashamed of it?"

"No. I just don't know if I will ever doctor again."

"Probably just as well. You couldn't stand the compytition. Widder Black does most of the dosin' around here. She don't kill more'n two or three a year with her messes."

"You aren't serious!"

Uncle Billy chuckled again, but his eyes were sober. "Shore I am. Some of her yarbs do good. Others are pizen. If she gives a mite too much —"

"She should be stopped!"

Uncle Billy covered a smile. "I s'pose a real honest-to-life doctor could stop her."

"So I walked into your little trap, Uncle Billy. Don't gloat too soon. I didn't come here to doctor."

"Course not."

But Dr. Luke had the feeling Uncle Billy had definitely got the best of that discussion.

"Do you think you can really get Cherish to clean? Won't it be awfully hard work for her?" Dr. Luke asked anxiously, but Uncle Billy only snorted. "Couldn't be no harder than choppin' wood and totin' water, way she does fer Jed." His eyes narrowed. "Jed'll be glad for her to come. He'd steal pennies from a beggar if he got the chance."

Dr. Luke fell silent on the way back to Uncle Billy's. Only once did he rouse from his thoughts, and that was when the old man shot a rabbit. "What a shot!"

"In this country a man's got t' know how to shoot."

It was strange how Uncle Billy's simple statement haunted him. Did the otherwise kindly old man think he needed to issue a warning? In spite of the warm sun, Dr. Luke shivered. He could see again the rising rifle barrel, feel the blow. Jed Hathaway, if it had been Jed who shot, wouldn't dare try again — or would he? Somehow in this remote place anything seemed possible.

4

By the end of the week, Dr. Luke's arm was improved enough for him to use it without too much difficulty. Uncle Billy set off early Saturday morning to see Jed Hathaway about Cherish's cleaning the old Lucas cabin.

"Can't you tell Jed I'll pay a certain amount? Then I'll pay more, and the girl can keep something for herself."

Uncle Billy shook his head. "Wouldn't do. First, where'd she spend it? Anything she bought at the store'd get back to her pa. If she came home with clothes or shoes he'd know." The old man took the broom straw from his mouth for a minute. "Now if you were to *give* her somethin' it'd be different, specially if it was somethin' small or that could be easily hid."

All the time his host was gone Dr. Luke thought. What could he give Cherish? What would a lame mountain girl like? He had no ribbons or frills such as Felicia used. They would be out of place anyway.

He was still racking his brain when Uncle Billy's faithful step sounded on the small porch.

"How did you do?"

Uncle Billy's face was a study in disgust. "He was drunk, as usual. Told him someone was a'movin' into the old Lucas place and needed it cleaned. Wondered if Cherish'd take the job." He paused to throw his hat aside. "The varmint said shore, she could come. Wanted to know what she'd be paid."

"Did you tell him?"

"I made it lower than you said. No use him thinkin' jest because you're a flatland furriner you kin be took."

Dr. Luke laughed at his protector. "What's a flatland furriner — besides me?"

"Anyone who ain't hill folk."

Dr. Luke was effectively silenced. But he couldn't stay still long. A vision of the lame girl who had undoubtedly saved his life rose in front of him. "Was she there — the girl?"

"Shore." Uncle Billy's face lighted a bit. "No bruises, either. Jed must've not got to his mean stage in drinkin' yet."

"There's got to be a way to help this girl!"

"I told you how. Someone'll have to

63

marry her. If I wasn't so old, I'd be purely proud to carry her home with me."

"You don't think Jed would let her live in someone's place, as a housekeeper?"

"You teched?" Uncle Billy's look rather than his words showed the impossibility of the suggestion. "You single and her livin' in your house?"

Dr. Luke flushed a dark red. "I guess I didn't think."

"Son" — there was a keen light in Uncle Billy's searching gaze — "I don't know how 'tis in the place where you come from, but up here there's certain things that ain't done — and that's one of 'em."

Dr. Luke tucked that away to digest later. "Will she come tomorrow?"

"Not tomorrow. That's the Lord's Day."

"I had forgotten. You don't mean to say Jed Hathaway keeps the Lord's Day!" Bitterness seeped into his statement. "I can't imagine him finding anything sacred or holy."

"Even if he don't, the rest of us do. You aimin' to go to church with me?"

It was the last thing Dr. Luke wanted. If God had forsaken him in Charlotte there was no reason to feel that same God would be found in such a place as Stump Hollow. He opened his mouth to refuse, closed it

64

again. "I suppose it would be a good place to meet the people who live here."

"If that's why you're goin', you may as well stay to home. Folks here go to church to meet God, not each other." Uncle Billy's wizened frame seemed to gain inches with new dignity.

"I'm sorry, Uncle Billy —"

But the old man had already gone out the door, leaving Dr. Luke staring after him, trying desperately to adjust to the strange new world he'd fallen into.

Nothing more was said of church until supper when Dr. Luke asked, "What time is your church?"

Uncle Billy relaxed from the silence in which they'd been eating. "Since we don't have a reg'lar preacher we jest git together the best time. Folks come in from a long way, so we meet at two and there's time for a bit of gossip before chores."

"Do the Hathaways come?"

"Nope. Jed's too ornery, and the gal wouldn't have nothin' to wear." Uncle Billy's grin held a bit of malice. "Womenfolk around here dress in their best. Not much soc-i-al life 'cept church." He must have caught Dr. Luke's answering grin, for he frowned. "Like I said, church is to meet God. That don't mean we don't enjoy folks afterwards."

"Church" was an experience Dr. Luke would never forget.

Uncle Billy served as leader. There were only two or three tattered Bibles, but those who had them shared. Uncle Billy read verses and made a few comments. Hymns were sung without books; everyone except Dr. Luke knew them all by heart. There was no piano or organ, yet voices blended. Later he would discover there had been a "singin' school" the winter before and folks had learned to sing "parts."

They were an interesting group. The women wore calico or, in a few cases, dresses of some dark material. Most carried shawls. The men were spanked up in well-worn clothing. The children peeked shyly from under sunbonnets or around their mothers' arms. Uncle Billy had told him most of them scratched out a living from the soil. Some kept hives and carried honey to Singing Waters. Those who raised chickens and cows sold eggs and butter to the tiny Stump Hollow store.

"Hard-working, industrious, but not too friendly," was Dr. Luke's first impression. Why should he care? Suddenly he knew he did care. He wasn't the type to be a hermit. He grinned wryly. After all, it wasn't as if he planned to stay.

Uncle Billy's voice roused him. Uncle Billy was a little unfamiliar in the dark suit that had obviously seen better days. It could have been the one he was married in. Certainly it was the one he'd be buried in.

"We have read the story of the prod'gal son. You all know I ain't no preacher. But I do have somethin' to say. S'posin' you had a good patch of earth like this feller did, and two sons to help plant and scratch it. Those two boys're different as day and night. The older one was good at workin'; the younger one was only good at dreamin'.

"You'd always told those boys when you were gone the land'd be theirs. But what if the young son comes and says, 'Paw, I got to see the other side of the mountains. Cain't you give me somethin' now, 'stead of when you die? I won't ask for nary a thing then.' Now, most of us wouldn't give it. But say we did. We sell off a piece of special land we been savin' and give the money to the young'n.

"We kin see him wavin' as he rides his old mule across the hogback an' out of sight." Uncle Billy paused for breath. Dr. Luke was fascinated, especially with the reverent look on the faces of the people sitting around him on hard school benches.

Uncle Billy took up his story. "So the young'n is gone. Me 'n' my other young'n tend the farm, git in a good crop. We hear tell from others who've been across the mountains how the boy who left ain't doin' good. Some city folk took his money. He couldn't find no job. Finally got one sloppin' pigs. So hungry he's been eatin' leftovers from the table that was meant for the pigs.

"One day while me and my other boy are plowin', a scarecrow comes marchin' 'cross the field. The young'n is back." Uncle Billy leaned forward and solemnly asked, "What we goin' to do? He done wasted money that'd of bought seed. But he's sick and wore out and starved." A big smile came over his face. "Why, folks, we're goin' to do jest what that feller in the Bible did. We may not have no fattest calf, but we'll cook up some greens and corn pone and side meat and take keer of that young'n."

Heads nodded. Dr. Luke found his eyes wet. Never in all the times he'd heard the story of the prodigal son had it made a deeper impression. Uncle Billy had told it the way a mountain man could understand — and they had.

"Say, Uncle Billy — what about that

there other young'n? The one who stayed to home?" The man next to Dr. Luke squinted up his face. "He warn't too happy, was he?"

"Nope, but he got over it. He couldn't understand how his pa could be forgivin'." Uncle Billy closed the Bible. "Don't you reckon that's how 'tis with us? We cain't forgive those who've done us wrong, so we cain't understand how God kin do it, either."

There were no other questions, and the "preacher who was no preacher" called for a closing song, then said, "We give thanks an' ask a blessin' on these folks and our crops. Amen."

Uncle Billy made sure Dr. Luke met the "folks," but they were hesitant. Was it his clothes? When Uncle Billy said folks wore their best he'd put on the good suit he'd brought simply because the little cottage was being sold and there was no place to leave it. Compared to the simple dresses of the women and worn suits or clean pants and shirts of the men, he was a dandy. Next week he'd know better. He didn't once think how strange it was to plan for "next week" when he'd only gone to church this time to keep from offending Uncle Billy.

That afternoon he restlessly said, "Think I'll walk up to my place."

Uncle Billy roused from where he'd been reading the Bible and dozing. "Find Hound and take him with you. He's good comp'ny."

Dr. Luke whistled up the dog and set out. So many impressions to take in! Just when he thought he had those mountainfolk pegged, they up and refused to stay in the holes he'd settled on. He'd been surprised at the cold meat and cornbread for dinner, washed down with buttermilk. Evidently Uncle Billy didn't believe in cooking on the Lord's Day.

How different it all was from Charlotte! The little suppers Felicia gave, regardless of the day of the week. The church with lofty spires in some imitation of an ancient cathedral.

"I got more from Uncle Billy's sermon than I ever did there," he told Hound. He was rewarded by soft dark eyes and a heavy body pressed against his leg. The growling dog that had greeted him his first night now followed him faithfully, having accepted him as part of Uncle Billy's life.

"He lives what he believes." Unbidden came the memory of a girl's shadowed eyes, her quiet voice, "I never pass a hurt critter." Then, "God'd not have me pass you by."

Now he asked the dog. "What could she know of God? Did the grandmother teach her? But if she was only four or five or six, how could she remember? How could she know much about God and keep it from such an early age?" He stopped short in the path. His eyes widened, staring not at the clump of flowers silhouetted against the crystal stream, but at something far beyond. "Is it because it's all she has?" His breath came faster. He could feel himself on the brink of an important discovery. "Hound, Uncle Billy seems to be the only one in this place who cares at all about her, and he can't do much. Is that why God's so important?"

The idea left him weak. He dropped to a flat rock by the small stream that rushed and tumbled across his land, thinking of the contrast between himself and the girl Cherish. For the first time he put aside his bitterness over what he termed "God's letting him down" to wonder. Had he ever done anything to deserve better at the hands of God?

The long afternoon stretched before him. Somehow he knew this must be dissected even as he had dissected so many other things in his work. He must see what it was that Cherish — and, yes, Uncle Billy — had that he lacked. It had been easy enough in Charlotte to blame God, to decide God had forsaken him. In the warm sunlight, with calling birds overhead and nodding flowers turning toward their Source, it was not so easy.

"I always believed in God!" Even to his own ears his spoken justification sounded like just that. Images from childhood replaced the early summer mountain scene. Himself, kneeling at his mother's knee, repentant over some childish wrong. His mother saying, "It is not my pardon you must ask, but God's. A broken dish, or a stolen cookie, or naughty word is not so important as a sin that stands between you and God."

How long had it been since he had knelt before God, repentant? The picture of a mountain "young'n" who had taken his inheritance and spent it in riotous living, then crept white-faced and sick back to his "pa," left him uncomfortable. Had he not done the same? He had been given the inheritance of salvation. He had accepted it, but had he ever shown to others how important it was? He had chosen to company with Felicia, who daintily patted fingers over a bored mouth when religion was discussed. He had busied himself in his work of patching men's bodies, but what of their souls?

"God, forgive me!" The cry seemed to burst from his throat but in reality only carried to the nearby sleeping dog, who roused and crept closer to Dr. Luke as if to offer the only comfort he could.

There in the little clearing Dr. Luke discovered what it was that had left him empty even in the midst of triumph; the reason ashes of despair remained to show where fires of success had once burned.

He had forgotten God. He had taken for granted the most precious thing in the world — the gift of Jesus Christ to him from Almighty God, to save him from death and give eternal life.

Suppertime was long past before he roused to realize darkness had stealthily crept into the hollows. Yet he lingered. "God, forgive me! I accepted your Son as my Savior, then got busy and forgot all about it. Father — I'm sorry."

The night wind sighed as fingers of peace crept into Dr. Luke's very soul. He closed his eyes, seeing the earnest, solemn little boy he had been, kneeling so long ago and inviting Jesus into his heart. A cry of gladness rang in the stillness as he threw his arms wide. He could hardly wait to tell Uncle Billy. But then he remembered Uncle Billy's remark. "We cain't forgive those who've done us wrong —"

Dr. Luke's joy subsided. Could he forgive Felicia and Jeffrey? Rebellion stirred, then was ex-tinguished by the great love he had felt moments earlier. "It's not going to be easy, Lord, but, yes, I will forgive them. If it had not been for what they did, I never would have come here — or perhaps never would have found You again!" A prayer of thankfulness welled up from deep inside. With it came a burst of happiness far greater than that he had had when he anticipated the head surgeon's post.

A faint rustling came from the bushes close by. Hound rose from where he'd been lying next to Dr. Luke and growled low in his throat. Even in the near dark, Dr. Luke saw the hair rise on his neck and back. "What is it, Hound? Who's in there?"

Hound leaped. A groan and a curse followed.

Dr. Luke parted the brush. A man smelling of whiskey lay before him. Vacant eyes stared at the match Dr. Luke had lighted.

"Name's Hath'way." He laughed, foolishly. "Goin' home."

Dr. Luke slowly iced. Hathaway. Jed Hathaway, father of Cherish. "Why are you here?"

The man looked surprised, tried to push off the restraining hand. "Told you. Goin' home."

Then Dr. Luke remembered. The Hathaways lived past his place, far from the carefully disguised still. Uncle Billy had pointed it out earlier.

"I'll help you." It was all he could do to convince the struggling man to stand up and walk. By the time he got him to the crazily pitched shack Jed had become a dead weight.

"Cherish." He kicked on the door, bent under Jed's frame. "I've brought —" he couldn't force himself to say "father" "— I've brought Jed home."

The door was flung open. In the dim light from a small fire he noticed she clutched a ragged garment around her. In spite of his anger at Jed, pity filled him. How she could stand it was more than he knew!

"Put him over there."

He followed her pointing finger and lurched across the cabin, unconsciously noting how clean it was, although shabby, even shabbier than Uncle Billy's.

"He'll sleep now." The husky voice straightened Dr. Luke from his position over the bed. Not trusting himself to speak, he motioned her toward the door, followed, and shut it behind him.

Daylight was gone, but the moon had risen. Her face gleamed in its pale light. "I'm beholdin' to you."

In sudden fury he grabbed her by both shoulders. "Why do you stay?" Contrary to Cherish's prediction, Jed had roused. A stream of curses, too vile to be heard, polluted the mountain air. Dr. Luke snatched Cherish close and carried her out of hearing. "Does this go on often?" Suspicion filled him. "Do you know what it means — the words he says?"

Even the moonlight could not hide the dull red in her face, the instant misery in her eyes. "I know."

He sat her on her feet, then followed as she dropped to a fallen log. "Why, why do you stay? Because he is your father?"

He felt, rather than saw, the imperceptible shake of her head. "No. Because I've no place else to go."

The hopelessness in her voice stopped him short, drained him of anger. "If you had a place to go, would you leave willingly?"

"Willingly!" A world of anguish was in her cry. "You don't know how I pray for someplace to go!" The next moment apathy blunted her longing for freedom. "It's no use."

Unable to control himself, Dr. Luke took one work-worn hand between his own. "Cherish, I don't know how, but I promise — I'm going to get you out of here if it's the last thing I do."

For a moment a wild hope flared in her eyes, only to die. "Don't be grievin', mister. When it gets too bad I run to the woods."

"But you hate him! Couldn't you — isn't there . . ." Something of her hopelessness rubbed off on him and dampened his determination.

"I don't hate Jed." Her face gleamed in the moonlight. "I don't love him, but I don't hate him, either. It's wrong to hate." Hesitantly she brought out the Bible she carried with her day and night. "It says in here to honor father and mother."

"Honor!" Dr. Luke couldn't keep contempt from his voice.

"I have trouble, but the Books says it. Jed really believes I killed my mother by

77

bein' borned. He says God made my leg crooked so's everyone would know what I did. He says I'm cursed."

"Cherish, do you think God would do such a thing?"

Eternity seemed to hang on her answer. After the harrowing of his soul the afternoon had brought, this incredible scene was totally unnerving.

"No." She lifted her face to the sky, where the stars seemed close enough to pick. "Granny said things go wrong when babies are borned. I reckon that's what happened to me. I know I didn't kill my mother. And I know God didn't mark me. It just happened."

Dr. Luke took in a ragged breath. How could she be so free of hatred, willing to accept her lot in life without complaint?

Her eyes were dark in the night. "Mister, if the Good Book says it, it's true. I don't know everythin' in it, but I do know God loves me. He sent His own Son to die for me so someday I could live with Him." Her face glowed. "If'n He did all that for me, I reckon I can trust Him for the rest."

The message of salvation from the lips of this untaught mountain girl rocked Dr. Luke. Yet there was something pathetic in the drooping figure. "Do you read your Bible a lot?"

"I can't read. But I confessed to bein' a sinner and asked pardon."

"Not at all?" He forced shock from his voice. "Then how do you know what's in it?"

"I remember some of what Granny said. And on the Lord's Day I sometimes slip around when it's nice and hide outside. Uncle Billy has the windows open when it's fair, and I hear him talkin' about Jesus."

"Were you there today?"

"Yes. I heard Uncle Billy tell about the young'n who went over the hogback. Someday I'm goin', too, but I won't ever come back." A faraway look crept into her thin face. "I don't know how I'll get there, but when it's time, the Lord will help."

Dr. Luke gasped at her total assurance. "You honestly expect God to get you out of Stump Hollow?"

"Of course. He led those children of Israel to the Promised Land after they'd tarried long enough to learn what He wanted them to, didn't He?"

Dr. Luke was speechless. He was unprepared for the simple faith of this child of the mountains.

Cherish went on, longing evident in every word. "You can read, can't you?"

"Why, yes." Must he feel embarrassed by her question?

"Do you read the Book every day?"

"Well — not every day." He tried to remember when he had last read the Bible. Had he been twelve or thirteen? There had been a memory verse contest and —

"If I could read, I'd read it every day."

Shame filled him. She must never know how lightly he had taken the Book so precious to her.

"I — I don't have a Bible with me." He saw her eyes open wide and felt reproved. "The one I had as a child got lost, and the big family Bible that belonged to my mother, it's hard to carry around, you know."

Dr. Luke was unprepared for what followed.

Slowly, as if bestowing riches, Cherish placed the worn Bible in his hands. "You can take mine, mister."

He blinked, trying to get rid of the mist that rose at her tone of sacrifice. "I couldn't do that. You will want it."

"I'd be gladsome for you to have it." She rose, standing above him like the wild creature she was. "You better go. Jed sometimes comes out after a spell when he doesn't go to sleep. Good night." She ran lightly across the partially cleared field, carefully avoiding stumps. Her limp didn't show so much in the moonlight, yet Dr. Luke was reminded of a wounded deer he had once seen, graceful but hampered by a dragging foot.

He stumbled to his feet and turned onto the trail from the long walk to Uncle Billy's. The little Book he had been given lay warm inside his shirt.

Uncle Billy was snoring when he arrived, so he slipped out of his shoes, gave Hound a last pet, and crawled into the loft. Sleep did not come easily. Again he was in the strange girl's debt. The something that had infringed on his consciousness now stood before him until he could recognize it.

A small smile curled his lips upward. He could feel his heartbeat quicken. He knew what he could do for Cherish Hathaway that would be more priceless than silver or gold. It would not be anything Jed could take from her — ever. He needn't even know.

As he drifted off to sleep, Dr. Luke's hand touched the ragged, faded cover of the only thing Cherish had to give.

5

Dr. Luke bounded down the crude steps the next morning. Uncle Billy was ahead of him. The coffee sent its welcoming aroma through the cabin, and side meat sputtered in the skillet. Dr. Luke noticed neither. He was too full of his plan.

"Uncle Billy, I know what I can give Cherish Hathaway."

Shaggy eyebrows rose in question.

"I'm going to teach her to read."

"Read!" The old man sat bolt upright. "How you aimin' to do that — and why?"

Dr. Luke hastily sketched in his experiences of the night before, omitting the soul-searching that had kept him out so late. "She gave — loaned me this." He produced the Bible. "If she can learn to read, it will be the greatest gift I can give her. And Jed won't know anything about it." Satisfaction oozed from every pore.

"Takes time to learn to read." Uncle Billy sounded doubtful. "Where you goin' to git enough time with her?"

"I'll pay her for so many hours, but use part of them to teach."

Uncle Billy's face wreathed with smiles. "That's mighty kind of you. I know she wanted to learn, but Jed wouldn't hear of her comin' to school when it started; said she was too old."

"She isn't. I bet in a few months she'll be able to read everything in here."

The watching eyes searched him. "Better know what's in it yourself before tryin' to pass it on." He got up from the table, reached for his own worn Bible. "Where you aimin' to start?"

Dr. Luke looked blank. "Why, where's the best place to start?"

The gnarled fingers turned musty pages. "Some folks'd say begin at the beginnin'. Now if 'twas me, I'd start with the New Testament. Not all filled with feuds and the like. Do the New first, then go back to the Old."

Dr. Luke marveled again at the many sides to Uncle Billy. The mountaineer's fingers were sure as they turned a few more pages. "For God so loved the world, that He gave His only begotten Son —" Uncle Billy looked up. "You believe John three sixteen, boy?"

If it had been one day earlier, Dr. Luke

would have hesitated, knowing he did believe, bitter against that same God. Now his face was humble. "I do, Uncle Billy."

"Good." The old man's face settled into laugh crinkles. "Reckon even a flatland furriner ain't so bad if he believes the Good Book."

The strangest reading of Bible verses imaginable followed. In spite of hiding twinkling eyes at some of Uncle Billy's pronunciations, Dr. Luke enjoyed it thoroughly. Something of Cherish and the look in her eyes clung to the old Book she had loaned him, and when the Bible study was over, Dr. Luke found his eyes moist.

The same thing recurred later in the day. He had insisted that Cherish stop her chores and eat part of the lunch Uncle Billy packed. Fascinated by her dainty eating habits, so out of keeping with the rough men's clothing she wore, Dr. Luke tore his stare free and said, "Cherish, I'd like to repay you for what you did."

Were ever eyes so innocent as hers? "You already have, mister." Long lashes covered the wood-violet eyes to sweep her cheeks. "You could've had Jed jailed."

"And you could just have let me die." Before she could do more than shake her head he added, "I just thought, while

84

you're over here cleaning —" he found himself suddenly shy, hoping she wouldn't be offended "— I have to stop and rest a lot until my arm heals. I need to — Cherish, I want to teach you to read."

He was totally unprepared for her reaction. Her eyes got bigger. Her face turned so pale he could see tiny freckles that normally were hidden by her wild rose cheeks. "Me, learn to read? Oh, mister!" The next instant two strong arms were around his neck. Two soft lips clung to his, then released as Cherish sprang up, color flooding her face, and ran lightly around the cabin.

"Cherish!"

But Dr. Luke's strangled cry received no answer. Cherish had disappeared as efficiently as she had done the day she sent him on to Stump Hollow.

Dr. Luke couldn't move. So unexpected had been the attack it left him speechless. When he finally was able to recover his wits he grinned. "Well, I guess she wants to learn to read, all right!" Beautiful, who was tethered nearby, brayed in agreement.

"Mister —"

Dr. Luke whirled. He hadn't expected her to come back so soon.

"I reckon the sooner we git this cabin

cleaned, the sooner you can start teachin' me." The only hint of her unusual actions showed in her heightened color.

It was the beginning of a totally satisfactory time period in Dr. Luke's life. He would have dropped the cleaning altogether in favor of teaching Cherish if she would have allowed it. She wouldn't. Only when he professed weariness did she put aside the mountains of rags and settle down to learn.

In spite of Dr. Luke's crude remembrance of how he first learned letters, Cherish caught on easily. As she worked she formed the letters, sounding them out. Windows were polished to the tune of, "A, aaaa; B, buh; C, cuh," while Dr. Luke corrected her accent without detracting from its charm. With only the Bible and his medical books to choose from, the old Book became primer, speller, even a basis to teach Cherish to "cipher" as Uncle Billy called it. In a few weeks Cherish could spell words. By midsummer she was reading. When early fall came and Dr. Luke could think of no more for her to do at his cabin, Cherish had a solid background. But what of winter? How could she continue to learn? She couldn't read or practice writing openly.

"But she must!" Dr. Luke paced the floor of his cabin. Uncle Billy had walked up for supper and to admire the spotless little home. "She's got the intelligence to become anything she wants. Uncle Billy, I have a dream for Cherish. She should go to Asheville or Charlotte and learn to be a nurse." His eyes caught fire. "I can teach her a lot this winter from my medical books! I caught her looking in them the other day and was surprised how much she already knows. She can learn, I'm convinced of it." He took a deep breath. "There's something else. If she were in a hospital, I believe her leg could be straightened."

Uncle Billy's excitement matched his own. "Well, wouldn't that be the Lord's blessin'?" His face fell. "It cain't be. Jed'd never let her go."

"Jed, Jed! The earth would be better off without scum like him!"

"Maybe so, but that don't change that he's her pa."

"When will she be twenty-one?"

Uncle Billy shook his head. "Like I told you before, she could be gittin' close, or it could be a couple a years."

"Would she know?" Luke was struck with another idea. "Wait!" He snatched from the shelf the old Book Cherish still insisted he keep. "Here!" His breath came out in disgust. "There's the birthday, all right. She won't be twenty-one until a year from next spring." Disappointment drenched his voice. "Jed was hanging around my cabin the other day, so I can't pretend there's more work to be done. How can I continue to teach Cherish?"

His problem seemed unsolvable. However, it was eclipsed a few days later by an incident at the store. Even the tiny store at Singing Waters seemed huge compared to the excuse for a store with its crooked sign nailed outside, Stump Holler Store. A few shelves of ancient goods, a few less bolts of calico, tobacco, ancient candy, and a big stove made up the inventory. Dr. Luke found it was the center of everything, especially on Saturday. The women came in for salt or sugar. The children gaped at the candy, and the men gathered around the big stove.

As a rule Dr. Luke avoided the curious stares by striding in for what staples he might need and exiting hastily. But this particular Saturday Jed Hathaway was lounging against the wall by the stove. Something in his posture halted Dr. Luke. Then he caught the words, "She may be my own flesh 'n' blood, but by —" he spit out a string of the rottenest language Dr. Luke had ever heard "— if she comes home with a brat from workin' fer him, I'll kill 'em both!"

For one second Dr. Luke was paralyzed. The next he lunged, narrowly missed the stove, and flung Jed Hathaway against the wall with a resounding crack. "You liar!"

Jed Hathaway crumpled to the floor without a word, a red stain beginning to seep from the back of his head.

"You've killed him!" The storekeeper gasped, but another lounger cackled. "Naw, he ain't dead. His head hit a nail on the wall."

Dr. Luke had been halfway to the door. He wheeled, the doctor ingrained in him conquering black hatred for the man unconscious on the floor. "A nail?"

"Yeah. That un." A dirty finger indicated a rusty spike pounded in the wall at a crazy angle. Dr. Luke shuddered as he demanded, "Are you sure he hit that?" Visions of lockjaw formed in his brain, images of those who died from such a wound. Was his response to the man's insulting Cherish going to end in murder?

"Git outa my way!" Big as he was, Dr. Luke found himself shoved rudely aside by a wrinkled crone dressed in dusty black skirts that dragged on the earthen floor.

"It's the Widder Black." The man beside Dr. Luke sounded awed. "If'n anyone kin save Jed, she kin."

The little old woman knelt on the floor and expertly raised Jed's lolling head. The stench of blood and whiskey almost turned Dr. Luke's stomach, even though he was accustomed to worse smells. "Bring me thet lamp."

Dr. Luke watched in horrified silence as the crone dipped her fingers in the soot mounded inside the chimney of the old lamp and started to press it to Jed's wounded head.

"*Stop!*" He reached her, shoved aside the black hand. "What do you think you're doing?"

"I'm aimin' to stop the bleedin'." Coal black eyes filled with hate glared from a walnut face.

"Not with that stuff." He glared back. "You," he ordered a gaping man nearby, "get me a pan of water, hot, and soap." His hands were already exploring the pockets of the lax man before him. He grunted when his fingers closed on a flask. "I'll need scissors, a razor."

"Who air ye?" If the black eyes had been

any sharper they would have torn him to ribbons.

"I am Dr. Edward Lucas."

His mind registered the shock that ran through the suddenly overcrowded store as his trained fingers accepted instruments, bathed and shaved the back of Jed's head, bathed again, then poured strong whiskey over the wound. His roving eyes fell on a length of muslin nearby. "Give me some of that — no, don't touch the middle!"

Only when Jed was showing signs of returning to consciousness did Dr. Luke look around. Disbelief, shock, hostility — the emotions on the open faces of those surrounding him ran the gamut. But he wasn't through. He carefully inspected the rusty spike. No trace of blood or hair. He checked the entire wall, found what he wanted — a splinter on the rough log, a tiny cluster of greasy hairs.

The breath he drew was ragged. "He'll be all right. He didn't hit the nail — just this." He rose from his examination and stood looking down on five feet of indignation.

"What right hev ye to come buttin' in where ye ain't wanted?"

Blue eyes clashed with black. "Was I supposed to stand here and let you kill him

91

with your witchcraft, then be tried for murder?"

The crone lifted a bent hand, shook her fist in his face. "I bin doctorin' in Stump Holler longer than ye bin born. Git out and stay out!"

"You don't scare me." Dr. Luke side-stepped her and the still-gawking crowd to march out the door, red-hot and aware of the whispers and malevolent stare following him. So that was the Widder Black, his "compytition." Rage washed through him. Must these mountain people die for lack of medical help? Must they be subjected to the "yarbs" of this terrible old crone who killed "only two or three a year with her messes"?

Out of sight of the store, Dr. Luke dropped to a stump, heedless of the rain pouring down. He was here. There was a need. Why not meet it? Since he met Cherish and Uncle Billy, something inside had cried out "home." Should he stay in Stump Hollow and use his calling as Dr. Luke for the good of these people? He still had some money left, so finances were not a problem — yet. Would the people accept him as a doctor, or would their superstitions prevent them from coming to him?

Any chance of continuing Cherish's education lay in ruins on the floor with Jed Hathaway. Why had he reacted so violently? Yet how could he have done anything else after those remarks about the purest girl he'd ever known? Would she hear about it? He fervently hoped not. To be the target of such cruel remarks was unthinkable.

Late that afternoon someone tapped at his door. It was Cherish. "I thank you for what you did at the store." Her eyes were almost purple.

"Did Jed tell you?"

"No. I was out of flour. I heard it at the store." Her delicate face colored.

"I hoped you wouldn't need to know." He caught her ice-cold hands, drew her inside. "Cherish, you know you can't come here anymore."

Her wonderful eyes were steady. "I know. Folks would think bad of me." Her lips trembled. "You don't think that way." It was not a question, but a statement. "Neither does Uncle Billy. He said I could come see him every day right at three and he'd read the Bible with me."

"And if I just happened to be there, too?"

Desire struggled with resignation. "No, Dr. Luke, it's best you don't come." Her eyes became like flooded flowers. "It's my fault, what happened today."

He tried to laugh. "Don't be ridiculous! It's the evil in Jed that caused it." He sobered. "I wasn't much better when I hit him."

Cherish only shook her head. "He asked me if I cared for you. I told him yes." A fury of passion filled her voice as words tumbled into the room. "How could I help lovin' you? No one but you and Uncle Billy has cared about me since Granny died."

Dr. Luke clenched his knuckles until they were white, but Cherish wasn't through. "Jed sees lovin' as dirty, sinful. He threatened to kill you." In her agitation she wrung her hands. One loose shirt sleeve fell back, exposing a white arm with a horrid purple and black bruise.

"Did he do that?"

Cherish pulled the sleeve back in place. "I couldn't get out of his way fast-enough."

"I am coming to see him. Tomorrow."

"No! You mustn't!"

Dr. Luke's jaw set like granite. "I am coming, and that's all there is to say about it. Go home, Cherish, or to your cave. Keep away from Jed. He will wake up with a raging headache. He will be mean. But

I'm going to be there first thing in the morning. The storekeeper said he'd haul Jed home. Remember, keep away from him!"

Could he ever push aside her white face and pleading eyes enough to sleep? Dr. Luke paced the floor for hours, trying to decide what to say to Jed. Reasoning was out. The man was beyond that. What would appeal to him? There apparently was no better nature in him. How could anyone stand the brute?

He fell asleep uncertain as to how he was going to bring it about but certain of one thing: the girl with the beautiful eyes and loving spirit must be rescued before she was destroyed by the madman the world called her father.

6

Dr. Luke had intended to go to the Hathaway cabin as soon as he got up, but he didn't. Only faint streaks of a winter dawn showed when he heard a pounding on his door. Groping for a robe to cut the chill from his unheated cabin once the fire went out, he fought sleep and finally got to the door. Dr. Luke recognized one of the men who had been in the store the day before.

"My woman. Widder Black said all there was to do was let her die and try 'n' save the baby, but —" The prominent Adam's apple rose and fell. "Could you help her?"

"Of course." Dr. Luke pulled the visitor inside and closed the door, noticing a light snow had fallen during the night. He rapidly crawled into heavy clothes and laced his boots, reaching for his medical bag as he dressed. "How far is it?"

"Jest down the Holler."

Dr. Luke found himself hard put to keep up with his leader's long steps. The man who said he was Sam Ryan walked as if his

96

heavy boots were cushioned.

"How long has your wife been in labor?"

"She said the pains begun yesterday mornin'. I fotched Widder Black yesterday evenin'."

Dr. Luke did a rapid calculation. He had already learned the mountain use of "evening" could be any time after noon. "When did the Widder say she couldn't do any more?"

"Jest before I come for you." Again the Adam's apple danced, betraying feelings Dr. Luke wouldn't have seen in the otherwise stolid man. "She cussed me somethin' awful, but I ain't gonna let my woman die if I kin help it."

Something in the man's natural dignity stilled the question "Why didn't you call me sooner, before Widder Black?" To the man parting branches so they could follow the footsteps in the snow made on the way over, it was a big step — going against tradition, perhaps even superstition. Only to save his wife had Sam Ryan dared do it. Widder Black's venomous face rose before Dr. Luke. So she had cussed Sam for "fotching" the doctor! He could well believe it.

When he stood over the disheveled, sweaty mountain woman, his heart sank.

97

She was too pale. He glanced at the old Widder, placidly rocking in a chair nearby, and nearly burst with rage. Only the presence of several big-eyed children huddled across the room held him back. "Sam, get them out of here." His eyes rested on Widder Black. "All of them."

Before she could protest, he took her arm and herded her out the door behind the others, ignoring her protests. "Sam, I'm going to need you." His level gaze looked into the very soul of the other man. "I'm going to be honest." His fingers moved with all their unused skill these last months. "Your wife is pretty bad. The only way we can save her or the baby is to operate and take the child. Even then —" He couldn't finish.

"She can't make it without yore cuttin' on her?"

"No." He made no effort to soften the blow.

"Then git started."

Never had Dr. Luke operated under such conditions. If it had not been for Sam's solid help it would have been impossible. But what seemed like hours later he laid a wrinkled, red mite into Sam's hands. "He's a boy." Then he turned his attention to Mrs. Ryan. She had come through the ordeal better than he'd expected.

He turned to see the gaunt man staring at the baby, trying to hide the smile forming beneath his moustache. "Is there a neighbor around to help for a few days?"

"Jest the Widder Black." The two men's eyes met again.

"I don't want her allowed in here."

"Whatever you say, Doc." The concerned face lost its smile. "Kin you tell me what to do?"

"I could, but —" Dr. Luke broke off, an idea forming in his brain. "Would you let Cherish Hathaway come take care of your wife for a few weeks?"

Sam's face dropped in horror. "She's marked! What'd it do to my woman 'n' young'n?"

Dr. Luke forced himself to stay calm. "She isn't marked. That's just a story Jed spread. She knows how to take care of the sick and hurt." He stopped. "Your wife needs Cherish. So does your son."

In the heartbeat of silence, Dr. Luke held his breath. Would desire to help his family be enough to outweigh years of superstition and prejudice?

"Fotch her."

Dr. Luke felt a wave of relief, followed by near panic. What if he couldn't get

Cherish, now the way was open? He had to, he thought grimly.

"Let your wife sleep as much as she can. I think I can have Cherish here in a few hours. And, Sam —" again that measured look of comradeship glimmered between them "— don't let Widder Black in this cabin!"

Sam's stumbling thanks followed him as he stepped back into the snowy world. On the way up and down hillsides he had been too preoccupied to notice how beautiful the world was. The light snow softened blackened snags, reminders of forest fires in the past. Some of the harshness of the mountain way of life was softened by the sugar-frosting. Dr. Luke breathed deeply. It had been good to get his hands on his instruments again!

"I can't get away from doctoring," he confessed to the sky. "I thought I could, but it's impossible." His mind jumped ahead. "What am I going to say to Jed Hathaway?"

He was no closer to an answer when he got to the shack. He quietly crossed the whitened expanse of now-dead garden stubble. No use taking chances of getting shot again.

"Miss Hathaway, I want to speak to your father."

100

Never had he seen fear as was in the girl's eyes — fear for him, he realized. Before she could speak he pushed past her. Jed was just sitting up, bloodstained bandage slipping from his unkempt hair.

"Sorry it was necessary to shut you up yesterday, Mr. Hathaway." Dr. Luke strode across the room. The direct approach was all he could use, hoping for success from the sheer shock it would bring. His ruse worked. "Here, I'll just take a look at that head." Probing fingers brought a curse to the man's lips, but not before Dr. Luke finished his examination, noting the wound was already healing.

"Git outa my house!"

Dr. Luke bit his lip and managed a laugh. "Not yet. We have things to discuss." He turned casually to Cherish. "By the way, Miss Hathaway, I delivered a son to the Ryans this morning. They'd like you to stay with them for a time until Mrs. Ryan is feeling better. Can you go?"

He intercepted her questioning look at Jed, now openmouthed. "They'll be glad to give you something for your trouble."

Greed overrode any other emotion in Jed's face. "Git, girl!"

Cherish snatched her too-big, hand-me-down man's coat and fled.

"Now, Mr. Hathaway, we can talk man to man." Dr. Luke dropped to a chair, marveling again at how clean the cabin could be, except for the man facing him. "Your daughter is a good worker. She could make a lot of money taking care of people." Forgetting for a moment whom he was facing, Dr. Luke let his glow of anticipation creep in. "If you'll give your permission for her to go to a hospital in Asheville or Charlotte, she can learn to be a real nurse. She can send money to you." He hated playing up to the grasping creature opposite. "You know how good she is with sick animals. People in the cities pay a lot for someone like her to care for them."

The liquor-soaked brain seemed to be considering. "How'd I know she'd send the money?" Evidently "money" was all he'd heard.

"Hasn't she always done what you told her?" Dr. Luke could tell he had struck home by the narrowing even more of the slitted eyes. Good! He'd milk it for all it was worth. "They'll teach her how to make money. Once they get her leg straightened, they —"

"What's thet?" Jed leaped from the cot, an insane light in his eyes.

"The doctors can straighten Cherish's leg."

"*No!*" The roar could have been heard clear to Uncle Billy's. "She's cursed by God! She kilt her own mother. No furriner's goin' to take thet away!"

Dr. Luke felt as if he had been hit in the stomach. Why hadn't he stopped while he was ahead? "But if she can walk straight, she can earn more money, and —"

"Not even fer thet!" Jed's gesture toward the door was magnificent. "Now git out!"

Breathing a prayer for self-control, Dr. Luke glared back into those fanatical eyes. "Then I'll marry Cherish and see she gets help."

"You try thet, and I'll kill you both." Jed literally foamed at the mouth as he snatched the rifle from the antlers on the wall, the same long barrel rising that Dr. Luke had seen that day months before.

"If you kill me you'll hang for it!" Dr. Luke struck down the rifle with a quick hand. "Uncle Billy and some of the others have had just about enough of you."

"Man's got a right to perteck his gal." Triumph bared yellowed teeth in a smile more terrible than anger. "So ye want my gal." Jed shoved his filthy face within inches of Dr. Luke's. "You kin have her if you want her so bad. I'll sell her to you!"

Dr. Luke's hands clenched to keep off the scrawny neck and leering face as Jed cackled, "She's right smart. You kin have her — fer three hunnerd dollars."

Unable to trust himself longer, Dr. Luke bolted, followed by Jed's maniacal laughter. By the time he got home he had been hot and cold by turns. Even the sight of an awkwardly wrapped ham with a crudely penciled "thanks Doc" failed to register, other than that Sam Ryan had evidently been there. Dr. Luke built a raging fire in the fireplace and shivered before it. From the sturdy crane he carefully lifted the kettle of hot water and made coffee, setting it in the coals. The idea of food nauseated him.

For hours he paced the hard-packed dirt floor. Why had God ever created such as Jed Hathaway? Yet Jed, as all men, had been created in the image of God. The fact he had chosen to become what he now was did not lessen the love God had for him. It was hard to reconcile. Yet Dr. Luke knew it was true. God loved Jed Hathaway, in his rebelliousness, just as He loved Dr. Edward Lucas — even when he had been so bitter. It did not change Dr. Luke's feelings toward Jed; it did change Dr. Luke's attitude toward God. Patient, longsuffering, always there waiting —

When he could no longer stand his own company, he tramped back to the Ryans. All was well. Sam wrung his hand and said, "The gal you sent is fine." Yet Cherish's smile only disturbed Dr. Luke more. He stumbled back into the night, crossed the hills toward home, and finally found himself turning into a familiar path.

Uncle Billy was waiting for him. "Thought you jest might be by. Come set a spell." He eyed Dr. Luke. "Have you et?"

"No."

Uncle Billy grunted. "Didn't think so. Reckon you've been too busy, from what I hear tell."

Dr. Luke came to life. "What's that?"

Uncle Billy ticked them off on his fingers. "Cut Mrs. Ryan and saved her and the young'n. Got Cherish Hathaway a-takin' care of them. Tried to get Jed to let you marry the gal. Gonna buy her fer three hundred dollars."

"News does travel."

If Uncle Billy caught the sarcasm in his voice he didn't let on. "Son, there's been more excitement since yesterday than there has been in a long spell. Folks jest nat'rly are talkin'."

Dr. Luke's laugh was short. "While they're talking, I wish they'd come up with some way to help Cherish."

The watching keen eyes deepened. "You'd really up and marry her to help? What'd she say about it?"

"I never asked. It just popped out when I was talking to Jed."

"If I know folks, an' I do —" Uncle Billy shook his head. "You goin' to buy her?"

"Uncle Billy!" Dr. Luke could feel his face crimson with anger.

" 'Pears that's the only way."

Dr. Luke sprang to his feet. "People don't sell their family! Other people don't buy them! How can you even suggest such a thing?"

"Some folks do. Them big plantation owners do it regular."

"Cherish isn't a slave or field hand!"

"Isn't she?" Uncle Billy's face was hard. "She's never been nothin' except that, ever since Jed brung her to Stump Holler."

"I can't buy her! I couldn't even if I wanted to. There's no way I could raise three hundred dollars, and if I could, do you think I'd be any better than a slave owner?"

"I saw a paper once where a feller bought some slaves then set them free.

Hmmm?" Uncle Billy's blue stare bored into Dr. Luke. "It'd mean her life, maybe. Jed's gettin' meaner all the time."

Uncle Billy hesitated, then slowly crossed to the mantel, lifted out a stone and reached inside. "I been savin' this. If it'd help Cherish, take it." In his palm lay a twenty-dollar gold piece.

For the third time that day Dr. Luke bolted into the woods. He gained speed until he was nearly outrunning Hound, who chose to race with him. But he could not run away from his thoughts. Incredible as it seemed, Uncle Billy thought the only way to save Cherish was to *buy her.* Doubt assailed him. Uncle Billy knew these mountain people. It must be the only way to protect Cherish, or he never would have offered money.

Dr. Luke groaned, catching his breath in the frigid air. His hands were tied. Yet what would happen to Cherish? Once she left the safety of the Ryans', wouldn't Jed take it out on her even more than if he'd never interfered? Maybe he should never have come here. He raised his face to the sky. "God, what should I do?"

His surroundings disappeared. He was back in Charlotte, agonizing over the treachery of those two he had loved more than life. That agony was gone — washed clean by acknowledgment of his own bitterness and resolution to forgive. He had been freed from his disappointment by the greater things that had come into his life: Uncle Billy, Cherish, Sam Ryan; most of all, his new relationship with his heavenly Father. What mattered now was the safety and happiness of the mountain girl who had saved his life.

So that was it. He had flung out his marriage proposal as a sop to Jed Hathaway, little thinking of how Cherish would react. What had Uncle Billy started to say when he stopped so abruptly? Suppose he should marry Cherish? The fleeting touch of her soft lips had stirred tenderness, called for protection. He'd never love her as he'd once thought he loved Felicia, but he would have the right to protect her.

"Rubbish!" His lip curled with scorn for himself. A girl like Cherish needed more than protection. She needed healing, then the chance to use her God-given intelligence.

And there was nothing he could do.

The helplessness that swept over him recurred often in the next two weeks. Every day he walked to the Ryan place, checked on mother and baby. Every time he avoided meeting Cherish's questioning glance, knowing it was a day closer to her inevitable return to the Hathaway shack — and Jed. Sometimes he felt as if he were walking a tightly strung wire over a bubbling cauldron of trouble, and again the helplessness overtook him. Was it the beginning of what he had protested to Uncle Billy against as apathy?

The day Cherish finished at the Ryan place he saw her for a moment, face pearly white against the old cap covering her bright hair. Was that face thinner? Was she dreading going home? He laughed at the word. "Home" in connection with Jed's shack was close to blasphemy. Her figure drooped as he watched her cast a longing glance toward his snug cabin, then disappeared in the softly falling snow.

A second time Dr. Luke was roused by a pounding at his door. This time it was Uncle Billy. "Come. She's hurt — bad this time."

There was no need for identification. Dr. Luke knew it was Cherish.

"She made it to my cabin, begged me to help." Sounds suspiciously like sobs tore from the old man's throat. "She ain't goin' back. If Jed comes for her, I'll kill him first, afore I'll let him git her."

Dr. Luke was silent. The grand old man was vengeance in person, and something in his voice proclaimed that was no idle threat.

Dr. Luke examined Cherish gently, then straightened. "No bones broken, thank God." He gazed at her discolored, terribly lacerated face and arms. "Her arms got the worst of it. She must have held them up for protection."

"She said she was asleep. Couldn't run. Jed called her awful names, hit her. She finally managed to git away when he fell over the stove."

Only once did she open eyes of stark terror, wildly look around the room, then sink back unconscious. For two days and nights the young doctor and old man watched over her, coming closer because of their shared sorrow. On the third day Cherish roused.

"It's all right. You ain't never goin' back." Uncle Billy's resonant voice evidently reached the seat of her fear. This time when she fell to the pillow it was into a natural sleep.

Later that day Dr. Luke stumbled toward his own cabin, body crying out for rest, soul for relief. Yet once there, his mind refused to stop its spinning. It was

110

fine for Uncle Billy to say Cherish would never go back to the shack. Carrying that out was something else. Uncle Billy must not kill. No matter what Jed Hathaway did, he was still Cherish's father — and important to God.

"No!" The vehement protest roused Hound, who had accompanied Dr. Luke home and now slept on the hearth.

"How could God send His own Son to die for men like Jed Hathaway? Was there anyone ever less in the image of God than Jed?" Yet as Dr. Luke gently opened the pages of the Bible Cherish had given him, John 3:16 leaped from the page in the flaring light of a final splinter in the fire.

It was true. God's Son died for all, even Jed Hathaway. Even though the man had chosen to stamp out every visible trace of God's spark.

"What am I to do? Oh, Father, what can I do?"

His own weariness was eclipsed by the sense of peace that stole from the Book still held tightly in his fingers. Cherish knew the God of the Book far better than he did. That God would open a way.

Days later a small boy knocked at his door. Dr. Luke recognized him as one of the Ryan children. "Letter come fer you."

He grinned. "To the store."

"Why, thanks!" Dr Luke glanced at the writing. Froze. Managed to smile. When the boy was gone, he staggered to the rude chair by the fireplace, staring at the writing he had seen so many times in the past — the writing of Jeffrey. He ripped open the envelope, not seeing a few smaller pieces that fell to the floor. It was short.

Dear Luke,

I know you can never forgive me. I don't expect you to. You gave up everything for me. I was crazed with fear, didn't know what I was doing. I walked off from Felicia — but dare not give up the hospital job. My mother would be sure to discover why.

I hope you won't misunderstand what I am enclosing. Something made me feel it should be sent. Use it for whatever you need most, and remember me as I once was.

Jeffrey

Dr. Luke cleared his throat, a wave of memories threatened to upset his balance. He reread the words "what I am enclosing . . . whatever you need most." As he stood to cross to the fireplace and restoke the

112

blaze, he noticed something lying on the floor.

There, faintly touched by one wintry ray of sun that had managed to escape long enough to light up his cabin, lay Jeffrey's enclosure: four one-hundred-dollar bills — more than enough to buy freedom for Cherish Hathaway.

7

Dr. Luke recoiled as if the money were a snake. How could he — yet like a voice from the past, his own prayer beat into his brain. Was this the answer? He laughed aloud, harshly, without mirth. He was getting as superstitious as the mountain people if he thought God would send money for the purpose of buying a human being.

"Rot!" Yet there was no denying the money had come. The need was still there. Jed had been lying low, obviously afraid of what might happen if Cherish died. Uncle Billy had let it be known she'd been hurt bad. Indignation swept the snow-clad mountains like winter storms. Yet in spite of newly awakened concern, Dr. Luke shuddered. What would Jed do next?

Would it be wrong to buy Cherish for the sole purpose of freeing her? He fought the idea for hours. He even decided it was impossible. Then he took the trail to Uncle Billy's. Cherish was sitting up for the first time. The discolorations were dimmer, but still evidence of her ordeal. Stronger was the fear in her eyes until she saw who it was.

"Come in, son. I was about ready to fotch you."

Uncle Billy's voice whirled him around. "Anything wrong?"

"Yep. Cherish saw Jed peekin' through the winder at her when I went to the store." His grave eyes met Dr. Luke's. "I cain't be here every minute."

Dr. Luke felt as if it had been taken from his hands. He tried twice, and when the words came they tasted metallic. "You won't have to, Uncle Billy." He cleared his throat, glanced at Cherish's white face. "I'm going to buy Cherish."

It didn't seem possible Cherish's face could get whiter, but it did. "Buy me!"

Dr. Luke wasn't to be stopped now he had decided. "It's the only way, Cherish. Jed will never let you go any other way. It won't mean anything. You will be under no obligation to me. You'll be free."

Something flickered in the violet eyes. "Free?" She gave a strangled laugh. "Free!" Color poured into her face as she repeated the word. She would have sprung from the chair if Uncle Billy hadn't restrained her.

"Cherish —" Dr. Luke could feel his

heart pounding "— would you like to be a nurse?"

Hadn't she comprehended? He tried again, uncomfortably aware of her staring at him. "You already know so much. If you would go to Asheville or Charlotte they would teach you a lot more. You could help folks instead of just animals. Why, the Ryans are singing your praises right here in Stump Hollow!"

"Couldn't you teach me?"

It jolted him. "I can teach you a lot. This winter you can stay with Uncle Billy, but anytime anyone calls on me I'll take you with me. I also want you to read, read, read. When you're ready I'll explain what's in my medical books. By next fall you should be able to get into hospital training."

"Mister —" her voice failed her, but Dr. Luke couldn't miss the light in her eyes "— you can't know how I've wanted to —"

Uncle Billy interrupted. "Better git some kind of paper when you pay Jed. That way it'll be all legal-like."

"I will." Dr. Luke's jaw set. He turned toward the door. "I'll be back later."

The tramp through the snow to the Hathaways was accompanied by a feeling of unaccounted-for doom. Why should he feel this way? He had the price Jed asked for Cherish, plus that other hundred-dollar bill safely in his pocket. Why should the whole dirty business leave him a little sick at the stomach? He was almost glad when the dilapidated cabin came into view. The sooner it was over, the better.

Jed was a little more sober than usual and evidently twice as mean. "What're you doin' back here?"

"I've come to buy Cherish." Dr. Luke winced, hating his conciliatory voice but determined not to antagonize the man who stood on the caving-in porch with his rifle. Even across the separating space between them he could see the crafty eyes light up with greed.

"C'mon in."

Moments later Jed stroked the largest bills he had ever dreamed of seeing. Dr. Luke carried away the paper he had written out in which Jed stated that for "certain considerations" he was turning over the care and responsibility and all rights to Cherish.

He did not go back to Uncle Billy's. Even though the other two would be waiting, he didn't want to see them — not yet. He climbed to the spot where on a twilight evening he had fought his battle and reclaimed the God of his boyhood years. Maybe there he would feel clean from the corruption he felt. Well, right or wrong, he had done what he thought best. The other money could be used to clothe Cherish when she left the mountains. It would also help pay part of her expenses when she got to Charlotte, for he had decided that was where she must go. Asheville was too close. Impossible as it seemed, Jed might take it in his head to cause trouble, and he wanted Cherish far away.

He sat for an hour, trying to figure how he could get the rest of the money needed to keep Cherish in training. With what he taught her, she could probably complete a good training course in less than a year.

Chilled to the bone, Dr. Luke headed for the log cabin that was more home than anything he had known since his parents died. The red glow of the dying fire leaped to life as he fed its hungry flames. Everything in it reminded him of Cherish — the cheap curtains, the well-scrubbed walls. A scrap of cloth she used as a handkerchief lay in one corner, unnoticed when he last swept his earthen floor. Maybe in the spring he'd put in a real plank floor, if he decided to stay in Stump Hollow.

Suddenly he knew he had come to another crossroads. It had haunted him for weeks, that unknown something just beneath his level of understanding. Now it was in the open. Would he stay in Stump Hollow? Nothing could have been further from his intentions when he first came, especially after seeing the prejudice, fear, and superstition of so many of the inhabitants. When had the first feeling of responsibility for those same people come — when Cherish risked everything to save his life? When Uncle Billy took the time to befriend him and teach him mountain ways? When he stood by Mrs. Ryan's bed and knew if he hadn't been there, both she and little Sam Edward would have died?

"No!" yet he could not shove aside the persistent thought. It haunted him as winter settled in, forming ice glazes on all it touched. It haunted him as a few more fearful mountaineers called on him for help. It took courage to go against the Widder Black. He could see it in their eyes. But these hardy people wanted their families to have a chance. His success with the Ryans had laid a foundation. A few more came, profited by the simplest suggestions, and went away to sing his praises. He often found food offerings when he got home.

He had made two deadly enemies. Once

when he was in the store he caught Jed Hathaway and the Widder Black in deep conversation and couldn't decide which hated him more. He shrugged it off and continued to teach Cherish. He was careful to give Uncle Billy a little money at a time, and the old man openly purchased cloth at the Stump Hollow store. Cherish made herself a dress after watching the other women, and when she walked into church the next week, a community gasp could be heard.

Dr. Luke did some gasping himself. Although he had always found her attractive, it wasn't until Cherish appeared in a little blue dress with tiny white flowers that softened her eyes to amethyst that he realized she was beautiful. She was accepted, too. The Ryans shoved over with broad grins to make room for her on the end of their bench, and Uncle Billy fixed a stern eye on his little congregation and said, "Reckon you all know my new daughter, Cherish."

Necks craned and Cherish's face turned red, then white, but after church was over, folks swarmed to her as if she were some new and wonderful kind of honey. Dr. Luke wisely held back and contented himself with smiling across the crowd. If there was talk about the way Cherish had been freed, he wouldn't add to it by being conspicuous in speaking to her. He noticed her limp scarcely showed under the full folds of her dress and two or three of the boldest single men in Stump Hollow eyed her. His brows drew together. He hadn't thought how this might come about. His anxiety was relieved as Cherish smiled shyly and impartially on all.

Winter finally ended and the creeks, streams, and branches rushed with spring runoff. Gardens were planted. The warm sun dried up the heavy rains, and flowers bloomed. Dr. Luke had never seen anything more beautiful than the miles of mountain laurel as he rode Beautiful through paths and trails. Although many of the old-timers clung to the Widder Black, he still had enough calls to keep him occupied most of the time he wasn't teaching Cherish. She kept her old clothes for riding, clinging to him as Beautiful plodded miles. She was almost to a point where he could teach her no more. He never had to repeat instructions. She learned rapidly, and her hands ministered as if they had been blessed with the gift of healing.

Spring droned into midsummer. Bees buzzed and birds chirped and sang. Yet in spite of the apparent tranquility of the land, Dr. Luke felt an undercurrent. Some of the faces that had once been friendly now turned away. Even Sam Ryan acted embarrassed when Dr. Luke rode up with Cherish to check on their family.

"Sam, what's the matter with you?" Dr. Luke asked in exasperation. "Not just you, but half the folks around. Am I poison or something? I haven't killed anyone."

Sam seemed to be struggling with words, but his innate honesty won. "Don't pay it no mind, Doc. There's those who're sayin' ye witched Jed into givin' up his young'n."

"You don't believe that!"

"Naw, but there's them thet do. It don't help none thet the Widder Black is addin' to it by cacklin' 'bout you 'n' Cherish." He nodded with his head to where Cherish was bouncing the baby on one knee. "I bin wantin' to tell ye, but didn't know how."

"Thanks, Sam." Dr. Luke gripped the toil-worn hand of the lank man, noting the faithful steadiness of his eyes. "I thought there'd be talk. I don't care, for myself. I just don't want her to hear it."

"Any fool kin see she's purely innercent. Let the rest clatter their gums."

Dr. Luke thought of Sam's advice as they rode back to Stump Hollow. He shrugged. It was all he could do. Evil-minded folks would believe what they wanted. Yet he could see a shadow in Cherish's face as he dropped her off at Uncle Billy's. She responded to his every mood, and he had been quiet on the way home.

"Anythin' wrong, Dr. Luke?" She had dropped the Mister as she worked with him, and her accent had lightened except in moments of stress.

"Nothing you can help by worrying."

The shadow did not lift. "Sam Ryan looked mighty serious. Was he — did he tell you what they're sayin' about us?"

His question, "How did you know?" was an admission.

"Folks hereabouts have been talkin' about me always. It's no different now." Two big drops formed in her eyes. "Except now you have to pay."

"They'll quit their talking as soon as you go off to school." He forced a smile. "Besides, you and I and Uncle Billy and God know there's no reason for anything to be said."

A poignant light replaced her tears. "I'm so glad you think like that." She slipped in the door, leaving him warmed by her smile.

"I'm going to miss her when she goes," he told Beautiful. The lop-eared mule just kept walking. But when they got to the edge of home he was startled. The front door of his cabin was standing open. He hadn't left it that way. He had learned his lesson earlier in the spring by coming home to find a family of raccoons in possession and flour and sugar strewn on the floor.

Had Jed Hathaway dared — Dr. Luke halted Beautiful a few paces back of the biggest tree in the yard and crept around the side of the cabin. He slowly raised his head and peered in the window.

"Ya-hoo!"

The next moment he was through the door, enveloping the man inside in a giant bear hug. "Jeffrey!"

Color returned to his visitor's face. "I take it I'm welcome?"

The last shred of holding back vanished forever, lost in gladness. "Welcome! I can think of no man on earth I would rather see."

His fervent assurance brought a look of total humility to Jeffrey's eyes. His grip was strong. "You're a better man than I am, Luke." His clasp tightened. "When I got your letter I thought I would —"

124

Dr. Luke couldn't wait. "Jeffrey, you'll never believe what I did with the money. I bought a girl."

Jeffrey's grip loosened as he stumbled to a chair. "You what?"

"Just what I said!" Dr. Luke laughed with joy. "And wait until you see her!"

Hours later Dr. Luke roused from the outpouring of everything that had happened to say, "We've got to eat, old man! But before we do, there's one more thing I want to tell you. When I left Charlotte I was filled with hatred and bitterness, not only against you, but against the world — and God." He raised his hand against the misery in Jeffrey's eyes, the protest he knew would come. "Now I can say with all my heart, I am glad it happened the way it did. What you did has brought the greatest thing in life to me."

"You mean this girl, Cherish?"

Dr. Luke's eyes widened. "Of course not, although she's part of it. I mean God." His voice dropped as he told of the terrible struggle he had gone through after hearing Uncle Billy's quaint telling of the prodigal son story. "I couldn't accept I would never find peace — even though I had seen myself as a sinner — unless I could forgive. Now I know it was at that moment the chains of disappointment, pride, and self-sufficiency began to loosen. Jeffrey, if you want happiness in your life, you must believe and accept that free gift of God — salvation. There is no other way."

"You never talked like this in Charlotte."

"I was a fool. I thought 'being good' was enough to assure me of hanging onto childhood beliefs. I was wrong. Those beliefs weren't a personal acceptance of Christ as Lord of my life and so weren't strong enough to help when things got rough." Longing was in his eyes. "At least I ask that you think about it."

"How could I help it? Man, you aren't the same person I've always known! That Edward Lucas was —" he spread his hands helplessly "— you are — it's as if you'd been born again! There's no other way to explain it."

"Even though I *was* born again when I accepted Christ as a child, I have never known the joy I found when I rededicated myself to Him, Jeffrey."

"Have you forgiven Felicia?" Jeffrey hesitated and doggedly added, "I learned she was as false as a rotten-hearted peach. She still comes around. She's even still beautiful — on the outside. But I don't want her. Do you still — care for her?"

"Absolutely not!" Dr. Luke's heartiness cleared the air of the final obstacle between them. "As far as forgiveness, she lives her life selfishly. I did the same before I came here. Yes, through Christ I've learned to forgive her — and glad I found out in time what she was!"

Jeffrey sat back down and leaned forward. The warm air of early evening shimmered on the doorsill, set to flame a bit of metal on the lamp on the mantel. "Luke, I was afraid you'd return the money. I never was one to pray much, but I prayed when I posted the letter. I'm glad you left a forwarding address. When your note came I felt I'd been forgiven, but I had to come to see for sure." Humility filled his face, and Dr. Luke rejoiced. "I've robbed you of so much! My mother's getting better. As soon as she's out of danger I'm going to confess the whole thing. You can come home, be given the post you wanted."

"No, Jeffrey. I've decided to stay here."

"Here?" Jeffrey's incredulous gaze rested on the crude furnishings, earthen floor, and homemade curtains.

"Yes." Dr. Luke shot a silent prayer skyward, hoping to make Jeffrey understand. "At least for now it's where I'm needed."

"Luke, beloved physician." Jeffrey smiled

at Dr. Luke's surprise. "I'm not totally ignorant of the Bible." He dropped his teasing, and a light crept into his face. "You say Cherish is coming to Charlotte for training and surgery on her foot? Why can't she stay with Mother? I've had a rotten time getting anyone. Mother refuses to have a 'companion.' If she knows Cherish's story she'll take her in and give her the mother Cherish lost long ago."

Dr. Luke's brain whirled. Was this another direct answer to prayer? "I don't have money for board and room, Jeffrey. I figured the extra hundred would pay for clothes and school. I have a little left of what I brought here, but not enough to help much. My patients keep me supplied with 'vittles' and Uncle Billy put in a double garden — said it was his 'contrybushun toward stoppin' Widder Black from killin' folk', but actually cash is short."

"Don't be an idiot!" Jeffrey's eyes snapped. "I'd have to pay a companion, Cherish will more than pay for her keep by being there." His excitement subsided. "I know you won't take money —"

"I don't need it for myself, just for Cherish."

"One of my uncles died and left a tidy

sum. Let me do this. It's the least I can do after getting your job." His eyes pleaded.

Dr. Luke responded to the pain in Jeffrey's voice. "All right. Now let's go give you a chance to meet her."

Uncle Billy was all smiles as he opened the door. "Reckoned you'd be su'prized. Feller said he knew you."

"It was the best surprise I could have had." Dr. Luke smiled at the old man. "Where's Cherish?"

"She run fer a clean apern when she saw you a-comin'."

"I'm here, Dr. Luke."

Dr. Luke turned. Cherish was in the little blue gown with white flowers. He opened his mouth to introduce Jeffrey and nearly strangled with laughter. Evidently Jeffrey hadn't expected a girl such as Cherish. For a long moment Dr. Luke looked at the mountain girl through Jeffrey's eyes. Not as the ill-clad benefactor. Not even as the competent helper who rode behind him on Beautiful. Simply as a girl. He was astounded. The glimpses of loveliness he had seen before melted into a rushing tide. He felt as if every blood vessel in his brain must burst. Cherish was no longer a child. She was a woman, pulsating with life, fulfilling her created purpose in beauty and innocence — and he was sending her away.

His long silence must have become noticeable, for Uncle Billy put in, "This here's Cherish, Jeffrey."

Dr. Luke caught Jeffrey's admiration as he took her hand. "Dr. Luke certainly didn't tell me enough about you."

Cherish only smiled, and Uncle Billy chuckled. "Takes a furriner to see the good in our mountains."

Dr. Luke drew in a ragged breath. The vision of Cherish as a woman had left him shaken. Calling on every ounce of willpower he owned he managed to say, "Let me tell you what we've been up to, Uncle Billy." But his eyes were on Cherish as he added, "It's all set. Cherish can go back with Jeffrey. His mother will keep her during training. It's a bit earlier than we'd planned, but it's the best way."

"You're comin' too?" Cherish spoke in a low voice.

Dr. Luke pushed back the exultant beat of his heart at the wistfulness in her voice. "Of course." How could he sound so matter-of-fact when his pulses raced? In all the time he thought he was in love with Felicia, it had never been like this. How could he have been so blind? Or had his love for Cherish been growing during the long months since he first came to Stump Hollow? "I'll show you around Charlotte, help you get settled in."

"I thank you." Cherish lost her questioning look and gave them a blinding smile. "Uncle Billy, Dr. Luke —" her eyes rested on Jeffrey, including him "— it's like a new world."

"Aren't you scared?" Dr. Luke asked curiously.

"Scared? No." Cherish rested one hand on Uncle Billy's Bible. "I reckon the Man who took care of me and saw that I got away from Jed will take care of me on the Outside."

Dr. Luke swallowed to hide his response and gruffly seconded, "I know He will." He deliberately changed the subject. "What are we goin' to do for clothes for Cherish?"

"Yore beginnin' to sound like one of us," Uncle Billy cackled.

But Jeffrey interrupted. "She looks fine now. Wait until she gets to Charlotte. She'll need certain clothing for her training. Mother can help her with that and whatever else she needs."

"Good idee." Uncle Billy squinted up at Jeffrey. "You live with yore mother, young feller?"

A wave of red stained Jeffrey's face, but his eyes met Uncle Billy's squarely. "No, sir. I have quarters at the hospital."

A look of grudging approval filled the blue eyes. It was there again a few days later as Jeffrey and Cherish set out on Sam Ryan's borrowed horses. Dr. Luke wasn't going. Uncle Billy's heart had been acting up, and Dr. Luke didn't feel he should leave.

"You won't overdo, will you, Uncle Billy?"

"Nope." He touched her hand as she stooped to kiss his weathered cheek. "Young feller, you'll take keer of her?"

"I will."

Dr. Luke saw the lips that had once been weak strengthen as Jeffrey promised, and a pang shot through him. Should he cry out the love he had for Cherish, plead with her not to go? Almost he gave in to his desire.

The next moment Cherish exclaimed, "I wish you were goin' with us, Dr. Luke, but oh! I can hardly wait to get there!"

Dr. Luke's confession died on his lips. Cherish's eyes were twin stars of anticipation. From months before came her voice, "When I go I'm never comin' back."

It was her chance. Nothing, not even his love, must hamper it. Jeffrey had agreed with his diagnosis. With surgery her leg might be straightened. As a beautiful, capable nurse she would be a far different Cherish from the one he'd known.

Dr. Luke bit his lip until he tasted blood. If he spoke now, her answer might be of gratitude. She had once said she loved him because he and Uncle Billy were the only ones who had been kind to her since her mother died. He wanted her love, but not based on kindness or gratitude. He wanted her love as a woman loves a man who is everything in the world to her. Until he was sure he had that, he would remain silent. After Cherish's leg healed she would go into training and see life far differently from anything she'd known. Then would be the time to offer her his gift of devotion.

"God go with you." Dr. Luke's blessing fell on the still air as Cherish and Jeffrey paused at the bend in the trail to Singing Waters, waved, and disappeared beneath the leafy green canopy dappled by maples.

Yet part of Dr. Luke seemed missing. He would have given everything he possessed to be the man riding off with Cherish far from the world of Stump Hollow.

PART II

8

When Cherish paused to wave at Dr. Luke before taking the bend in the trail to her new life, she was unprepared for the rush of feeling sweeping over her. It threatened to unseat her from her awkward perch atop the horse's swayback.

Behind lay years of her life. She raised her face to the ridges that faded into higher hills, blue and smoky in the distance, covered with the peculiar substance that gave them their name. A verse she and Uncle Billy had read only this morning from Psalm 121 came to mind. "I will lift up mine eyes unto the hills, from whence cometh my help. My help cometh from the Lord." For one moment she wanted to clamber down from the horse, run back to Stump Hollow, and stay, in spite of the years of unhappiness she had known there.

Something of her feelings must have shown in her face, for Jeffrey quietly said, "He wants you to go."

She started, flushed. "I know."

"You can always come back. If you do, you'll have skill to help them. You'll have strength to walk straight, run faster, be free."

Jeffrey would never know that the one word *free* saved her. Her earlier anticipation returned; Stump Hollow and Uncle Billy dimmed a bit. "What's it like in Charlotte?"

"Busy. You'll see buildings, more than you've ever seen before."

"That won't have to be many," Cherish put in with a rare flash of humor.

Jeffrey laughed with her, admiration clear in his eyes, even for the quaint figure she presented. Her little blue dress was in a saddlebag, to be donned after the wagon ride from Singing Waters to Asheville. For now the drooping big hat and old, men's clothes served as riding habit. Even in them she had a certain charm.

"I can hardly wait for Charlotte to see you."

"Don't you mean for me to see Charlotte?"

"Not at all." Jeffrey shook his head vehemently. "You're going to be a sensation in Charlotte. Just wait until my mother gets through with you! There won't be a girl there who will be able to come close to competing."

"I don't know what that means."

Under the clear gaze of the mountain girl Jeffrey hesitated, then laughed. "Just remember I saw you first." He cocked his head at her. "Was it hard leaving Dr. Luke?"

Cherish rode silently for a long way. Jeffrey was learning she never answered until she knew exactly what she was going to say. There was no guile in Cherish — she had the innocence of a child.

"I reckon it was the hardest thing I ever did." Her unconscious sigh told more than her words.

Jeffrey was ashamed for asking and quickly turned the subject by asking her what kind of trees were clumped along the trail. Her explanation lasted until the shadow on her face from remembering lifted.

When Cherish reached Asheville, she litterally clung to Jeffrey. "Why, I've never seen so many folks at once!" She clutched the blue dress she had changed into.

Jeffrey looked down, pity in his eyes. There couldn't have been even a hundred people at the train depot. He carefully camouflaged it by telling her, "Wait until the train comes."

It was a thrilling moment. Cherish

stared round-eyed at the fire-breathing, self-important monster that belched its way into the station on twin shining pieces of metal Jeffrey said were tracks. "We aren't goin' on that!" Her eyes begged for reassurance.

Jeffrey took the small, trembling hand in his big one. "I won't let anything happen to you, Cherish. I promised Uncle Billy."

Cherish forced herself to release the breath she had been holding. With her free hand she smoothed a wrinkle out of her dress and looked anxiously around. No one seemed to be paying any attention to her. Besides, hadn't she boasted God would look out for her? By the time she and Jeffrey were seated in the train, her heartbeat had slowed to only slightly above normal. There was a bad moment when with a loud whistle and sharp jerk it started, but once they were on their way, Cherish found it wasn't so bad. Jeffrey had given her the window seat. It was all she could do to keep from exclaiming as cows galloped past, buildings appeared and disappeared by magic, and fields sped by.

Some innate sense of the fitness of things saved Cherish from embarrassing herself on that first train trip. Always a little shy around strangers, she didn't blurt out things that would have given her away. A few times she caught the look of admiration Jeffrey gave her. She couldn't know her violet blue eyes sparkled and the shiny brown hair neatly tucked under a braid only enhanced the red of her cheeks.

"Cherish, you may want to wear your hair differently when you get in training. Your braid won't go under the cap very well."

"I'll do whatever they tell me." For a moment determination took precedence over her excitement. "I aim to be the best nurse in North Carolina."

"You probably will be." Jeffrey sounded sincere. "Dr. Luke tells me you've already studied everything in his books."

Her eyes glowed. "It's so wonderful how God made all the parts of a body so they'd work together, isn't it?"

"Yes. Yes, it is, even though I've never thought of it that way."

She looked astonished. "You never thought about God makin' folks?"

Embarrassed, he confessed, "I guess I've been just too busy to pay attention to God."

Cherish withdrew to the window, watching the rising color in his face. "If I had been too busy for God I guess I'd just

have up and died. I couldn't of — have —"
She was carefully trying to correct her language as Dr. Luke had taught. "Anyway, God's all that kept me goin' when Jed got mean."

Jeffrey was silenced. When he did speak, Cherish could hear longing in his voice. "Maybe someday you can teach me about your God."

"No one can do that. You have to listen with your heart when He speaks."

"You believe God speaks?" There was no mistaking Jeffrey's surprise.

"Of course." Cherish might be on unfamiliar ground about towns and trains, but not about God. "Haven't you ever walked by a branch and heard God singin' in the water? Or heard Him callin' in the thunder? Why, you don't know what you've missed! Sometimes He speaks in the wind, or through baby birds. Most of all He speaks inside." She fell silent, seeing Jeffrey did not understand. "I guess maybe it's so noisy down here in the Outside, folks can't hear God very well."

"Cherish, don't ever change!" Jeffrey impulsively placed one hand on her arm. "You'll learn a lot here, but don't let it change you."

Sheer innocence shone in her eyes. "I

reckon I'll never learn to understand everything there is to know. I do know God is here, too."

If Asheville had been frightening, Charlotte was an ordeal for the sensitive girl. Crowds of people were waiting for the train. A band was playing in celebration of some local holiday. Everywhere Cherish looked there was something distracting. After she and Jeffrey were helped into a carriage, she looked sober. "I see now why you can't hear God. I was right, wasn't I? It's too noisy."

She looked so young and unprotected Jeffrey couldn't help repeating, "Don't be afraid, Cherish. I'll take care of you."

Another carriage had drawn alongside. A mocking voice cut into their conversation. "Well, Jeffrey, and what have we here?"

Cherish looked up in amazement. Of anything she had seen since leaving Stump Hollow the woman leaning from the other carriage was the most startling. Her bright green dress was cut low, so low that Cherish gasped. Uncle Billy had told her city folks dressed differently, but this woman's dress was shocking. Even the folds of fluffy white stuff didn't cover the bare flesh gleaming through. Long golden hair coiled in fantastic shapes, writhing the way Cherish had once seen a group of baby snakes do. But the look in the green eyes, hard and cold, reminded Cherish even more of those snake eyes in Stump Hollow.

Jeffrey finally found his tongue. "Miss Temple, Miss Hathaway."

The green eyes raked Cherish, dismissed her as insignificant. "I wondered where the great Dr. Carr had been. It seems he was strangely missing from the ranks of his hospital when I checked." She shrugged her shoulders, allowing the frothy stuff to slip even lower. "Drive on, Sam."

"Yes'm." The driver rolled his eyes skyward, touched the reins and the carriage moved ahead, leaving Cherish staring after it. This time she couldn't restrain herself. "I never knew folks to go out in broad daylight undressed!"

"Cherish —" Jeffrey sounded more sober than she had ever heard him "— have nothing to do with that woman. She runs in and out of the hospital as some relative is on the board. If you see her coming, get out of her way. She is evil."

Cherish shuddered. "She looked like our snakes back home."

"She is, only more deadly. Someday I may tell you just what she really is." He drew up to a house. "This is my mother's house."

"How grand," Cherish whispered, noting the neatly painted white house and well-kept garden.

Jeffrey looked at the tiny cottage, started to speak, and stopped. Then, "Let me help you down."

Cherish smoothed her dress again. "She doesn't know you're bringin' me. What if she says I have to go?" Her hands trembled.

"She won't." His confidence restored some of Cherish's poise as he flung wide the door. "Mother, I've brought you someone."

Cherish held her breath. A small woman, merry face set in a little white cap, threw wide the door. "Well, Jeffrey, and what have we here?" The same words that woman, Miss Temple, had used but with what a difference! "Come in, child! Jeffrey, close the door. The mosquitoes have been trying to get in." She opened her arms. "Welcome, child."

"Why, you're like my own Granny!" Cherish flew straight to the little woman who hugged her and said, "Bless my soul! You're no bigger around than a broom handle. I'll get some meat on your bones."

She pulled back. "What's your name, child?"

Cherish couldn't get a word out past the lump in her throat. All the worry and fear of new things since leaving Stump Hollow culminated in a bright tear that escaped to drop on the old woman's wrinkled hand.

"Her name is Cherish Hathaway," Jeffrey explained, eyes meeting his mother's in a long glance. "She comes from a place called Stump Hollow. She saved Dr. Luke's life. Now she wants to train to be a nurse, if she can stay here with you."

"As long as she likes." Mrs. Carr turned back to Cherish. "You look tuckered out, child. Good thing I changed the sheets on the spare bed today. The good Lord must have been letting me know company was coming."

It was the one touch needed to erase forever any feeling of strangeness. Cherish's face took on an almost holy look. "Oh, you know the good Lord, too?"

"Indeed I do." Her lips compressed. "I just wish that son of mine would — but no time for that. Come." She led Cherish to a tiny room at the back of the house. Just a white bed with a colorful patchwork quilt, white-painted walls, a window that gave a view of a distant hill, and a curtained-off place for clothes. "It's not big, but it should do. We'll get a table if you want to study in here, though I'd be right proud to have you study out by the fire. My knitting needles don't make much noise."

Touched by the wistfulness in her voice, Cherish broke her reserve and pressed her lips to the withered cheek. "It's the most beautiful room in the world, and I'm obliged."

"There, child." Mrs. Carr bustled out and returned with a pitcher and basin, a dish of soft, sweet-smelling soap, and a big white towel. "Freshen up, then get some rest before we eat." She paused in the doorway. "Are your things in the carriage?"

Cherish's laugh was a little hysterical. "I don't have any things, just what I have on."

Mrs. Carr didn't bat an eye. "Then you'll need a gown." Again she hurried away, this time bringing back a thin muslin gown with short sleeves. "You can use this for sleeping." She helped Cherish unfasten her dress and smiled. "Sleep as long as you can. Train travel is always tiresome." As she closed the door and Cherish dipped into the warm water, the tired girl dropped to her knees. "This must be what heaven's like." For a long time she stayed on her knees, too tired to pray, letting her spirit drink in the peace of the room. At last she rose, washed, and slipped into the gown and bed. She was asleep almost before her head hit the pillow.

In the little kitchen Mrs. Carr set about preparing the daintiest supper she could while the stranger-girl slept. "Where did you ever find her, Jeffrey? I know what you said, but I didn't know our mountains grew any girls as rare as this one. Cherish, you say her name is?"

"Yes." Jeffrey stretched, then straddled a chair. "Her mother died in childbirth. Her father hates her for 'killing her mother.' He told everyone that the girl's crooked leg was God's punishment for being a murderer." In a few well-chosen words he described the things Dr. Luke had shared. "Her father is the worst element of the mountains. Not that we don't have the same here. We do. But Jed Hathaway doesn't deserve to live. I don't know why God hasn't struck him down years before this."

Faded blue eyes searched his. "Perhaps for the same reason He doesn't strike the rest of us down when we are rebellious."

Jeffrey dropped his eyes. "I'm going to make arrangements at the hospital tomorrow to see if we can't fix that leg." He rose to pace the kitchen. "She needs love and care, Mother. Am I asking too much, with your heart condition?"

"Jeffrey, I believe God sent her. Just a few days ago I was wishing I had someone. You're so busy at the hospital, especially since you were named head surgeon. Sometimes I wish it had gone to someone else. You seem so tired all the time." She smiled. "I think we were happier when we struggled — I don't always fit in here." She added quickly, "Not that I'm complaining. I'm just glad she came."

Jeffrey froze in place, but she wasn't through.

"She's lovely, you know. Not like that Miss Temple who came here inquiring about you." Probing eyes demanded an answer.

"I don't see Miss Temple except when she comes to the hospital, and not then if I can help it."

Mrs. Carr breathed a sigh of relief. "Good. She drives around as no decent woman would do. Such a difference between her and the little one you brought! I wonder how they will react to each other?"

Jeffrey laughed. "They already have. Felicia was insolent, Cherish astonished. She couldn't understand how any girl or woman would undress so in public." He laughed again. "I have to agree with Cherish now I'm free of Felicia's wiles. I can hardly wait to see how Felicia acts when she sees Cherish in something other than her homemade dress."

"You aren't going to make a fashion plate of her!"

"No, Mother." He stopped his teasing. "I'm going to let you dress her the way you would have dressed the daughter you always wanted."

"Son —" there was a tremor in her voice, pleading in her blue eyes "— is there a chance she might be my daughter — someday?"

The kitchen was so silent the purr of the cat on the fireplace hearth sounded loud.

"No, mother." Jeffrey was no longer smiling. "I don't think Cherish even realizes it yet, but she loves Dr. Luke." Pain filled his face. "I will never do anything to change that."

His mother's eyes never left his. "How does your friend feel?"

"I believe he discovered just before she left what he has felt all the time he has been in Stump Hollow."

"And he let her go." Mrs. Carr's white-covered head nodded. "Laddie, if he loves her enough to let her go, this Cherish is blessed above many women."

"Someday she will go back to him." Jeffrey forced a smile. "I won't say I'm not charmed by her. But I'm not going to fall in love with Cherish. I gave Uncle Billy my word of honor to care for her, and that's just what I'm going to do."

They talked while the chicken stewed, while the little white dumplings and fresh green peas from the garden cooked. Even while the gingerbread cooled in the window, neatly covered with a piece of netting. And just as summer was beginning to overcook, the door of the little white room opened and Cherish crept out, wondering if she had dreamed the whole thing and would wake up in the cave at Stump Hollow.

9

"It's all set!" Jeffrey burst into the little white cottage, face gleaming. "Why, Cherish —" He broke off to stare. "Whatever have you done to yourself?"

Cherish felt herself flush. She smoothed down her little blue dress, touched the lacy collar Mrs. Carr had given her and then her hair. "It's what your mother has done." She peered anxiously at Jeffrey. "Do you like my hair this way?" One hand felt the smooth expanse where Mrs. Carr had tamed the rebellious curls into a wave, ending in a neat coil at the back of her neck. She had peeped at herself in the mirror and wondered if the girl whose hair was neatly parted in the center to show off a high, white forehead was really Cherish Hathaway.

"It's perfect." Jeffrey laughed. "It will fit under a cap, too."

His mother beamed. "That's just what I thought. She won't be needing dresses for a time, until you get her all fixed up. By

152

then I will have some made for her."

Jeffrey stopped admiring Cherish long enough to tell them, "It's all set. We operate on your foot tomorrow." His eyes were grave. "Dr. Luke explained it to you, didn't he?"

"He said there was a big lump there. It was pushin' on something and my foot just naturally turned crooked to keep from hurtin'."

"That's really about it. Didn't you ever notice the lump?"

"Of course." Cherish's voice was low. "But what good would makin' a fuss have been? Jed wasn't about to do anything." There was no bitterness in her voice, only resignation. "Besides, Dr. Luke said the lump was probably there when I was little and has kept growin' since then." Her fingers probed the spot, tender now that she had on an old, too-big pair of slippers that rubbed against it. "Dr. Luke said 'twasn't my leg that was twisted at all, but my foot."

"That's right. We're going to remove that lump, Cherish." Jeffrey swallowed hard. "If all goes well, you'll be able to walk straight when the wound heals."

"Kind of like takin' out a bullet?"

"Yes, except this will be attached inside your foot." Jeffrey was having a hard time explaining without frightening her.

"Dr. Luke said you're a good man and doctor and I was to trust you."

"Thank you, Cherish." His voice was husky.

"How soon can I have my girl back?" Mrs. Carr demanded. "She promised to draw some of the quilt patterns the Stump Hollow women use so I can get started on something different."

"Sunbonnet Girl, Flower Garden, Rising Sun." Cherish flashed a quick smile. "I don't know which is the prettiest."

Jeffrey hesitated. "She should be able to come home in a few days." He fixed a stern gaze on Cherish. "You'll have to stay off your foot. When the wound is healed, I'll put splints on to help get your foot back to normal faster."

"Whatever you say." Cherish was docile. "God must have sent you just when I needed someone." Cherish struggled to get her feelings into words. "Even after Dr. Luke bought me I didn't see how I could come here. I'm obliged."

Jeffrey swallowed again, but his mother said, "I'm the one who's obliged. I'll be praying — for both of you."

Cherish moved through her first full day in Charlotte as if in a trance. Tomorrow

154

she would see the hospital where Jeffrey and Dr. Luke had worked together. Once she asked, "Why did Dr. Luke leave here and go to Stump Holler?"

Mrs. Carr shook her head. "Something about an accident."

Cherish caught the flash of pain on Jeffrey's face. Suddenly the fevered ramblings of long ago when Dr. Luke was hurt made sense. Her keen eyes turned away from the betraying pallor in his expression. So that was it. Dr. Luke had taken the blame for something Jeffrey had done. Something warm swelled within her, along with pity for Jeffrey. His mother didn't know, so it must have been between the two doctors. Before the silence could grow uncomfortable she asked, "Can — may I see the hospital before you fix my foot?"

Relief mingled with the cloud in Jeffrey's face. "Of course. They all know you're coming. Just do as I tell you."

"Of course."

It wasn't hard. Once they stepped inside the large building, white-painted outside, so busy inside, the Jeffrey she knew disappeared. In his place was a stranger — efficient, respected Dr. Carr.

Cherish's eyes grew wide as she noticed

nurses covering patients, carrying bandages, walking easily yet rapidly to get their work done. "Will I look like that?" Her voice was almost reverent as she pointed to a young woman dressed in a long gray gown, sparkling white collar and cuffs on her long sleeves matching the big apron Jeffrey said was called a pinafore.

"Hardly." He chuckled at her disappointment. "You'll dress like that, but you'll be much prettier."

"I hope I can learn everything." She was sobered by the weight of responsibility suddenly dropping over her.

"You will have to study hard." Jeffrey looked into her anxious face. "But you want to learn so much it will overcome what you lack."

Only once did Cherish balk. She had been put to bed, and a curtain was drawn around the bed, giving a little privacy from the others in hard cots up and down the great room. Jeffrey came in with a flask and glass. He poured amber liquid into the glass. "Cherish, I want you to drink this. It will help dull the pain."

She obediently took it and raised it to her lips. Her hand froze. She shrank back, eyes wide. "No! It's moonshine."

"It isn't moonshine," Jeffrey patiently explained. "It's brandy."

"It smells the same."

"We use it to help the pain." His eyes pleaded with her, and the nearby nurse fixed a curious stare on the new patient.

"I can stand the pain." Cherish shook her head stubbornly. "But I won't drink that, no matter how awful the pain gets."

In vain they tried to change her mind.

She was adamant. "Do what you have to. I'll stand it."

Great beads of sweat stood on Jeffrey's forehead as he ordered the nurse to swab the poor, twisted foot. His fingers trembled as he picked up the shining scalpel, hesitated, then set his lips and made the first cut. Cherish never flinched. Once Jeffrey glanced at her, seeing her pearly white face and a bright spot of blood where she had bitten her lip to keep from crying out, the same lips silently moving in what must be prayer. The round-eyed nurse followed instructions, never taking her eyes off Cherish.

"She's fainted, Dr. Carr," the nurse informed him.

"Good." With a final thrust he pushed the scalpel deeper, lifted, cut again, and removed a bloody, walnut-sized piece of material. Blood spurted, but the nurse was ready with soft cloths.

"Hand me the whiskey." Jeffrey liberally drenched the foot, pressed cloths again, this time binding them tightly. Over them he put a great wad of cotton wool. Not until it was over did the nurse venture, "Is she some kind of fanatic? Why wouldn't she drink the brandy?" Grudging admiration shone in her eyes. "I never saw such a Spartan."

"She's seen too much of the bad effects of liquor." Jeffrey stood abruptly from the chair he had dropped into. "Let's bring her around."

Cold cloths on Cherish's forehead brought a fluttering of long lashes against the pale cheeks, then great violet depths. "Is it — over?"

"All done." Even through the haze surrounding her Cherish could hear the relief in Jeffrey's voice. "We took out a lump the size of a walnut. It's no wonder you couldn't walk straight."

"Is — can I sleep now?" Cherish felt drained.

"Sleep all you can."

Cherish heard no more. When she opened her eyes again it was to be aware of a throbbing foot and mouth so dry she couldn't swallow. She moved restlessly, being careful to keep her foot still on the pillow someone had placed under it.

"Drink this." Something cold and slightly salty slipped down her throat. She looked into the kind face of the nurse bending above her, sponging her face with a damp cloth.

"You must be an angel."

"No. Just a nurse." The young woman leaned back. "You'll be doing this in a few months."

For the next few agonizing days that was all Cherish could hang onto, except her belief God was watching after her. Her foot hurt incessantly. The lump had been bigger than anticipated. The few days Dr. Carr had predicted stretched into more than a week. Several times his mother came in to visit.

On one of those visits she said, "You're the talk of the hospital, you know." Her eyes twinkled. "Everyone is stopping me to tell what a model patient you are, even if you wouldn't drink the brandy."

"I couldn't."

"I understand." The older woman's eyes were soft. "Your room is waiting. It won't be long now."

Jeffrey had to carry her in from the carriage when she went "home." He had rebandaged the wound with a new dressing and was elated over the progress. "It's quit draining. A few more days and we'll splint it."

To the active girl the weeks with splints were nearly unbearable. "I can't walk as well as I did before!" she commented, then laughed. "But I will."

"Of course you will."

A cloud dimmed her brightness. "I can't start trainin' when I was supposed to, can I?"

Jeffrey shook his head, sympathy in his face. "No. You'll wait and start next spring. This winter you can look after my mother. She needs you."

His artful camouflage of the time she might have considered wasted worked. Cherish brightened up immediately. "That's right. I can still study, too, can't I?" Practically every trace of her mountain word usages had vanished. Dr. Luke's months of teaching had paid off.

"You'll be so far ahead of your class they'll be jealous. First, let's get you completely well."

By November Cherish was walking a bit every day. By December she was running through the fields near the Carr cottage.

One day Mrs. Carr said, "Cherish, would you call me Mother?"

Rosy-faced from a run, Cherish dropped by the old woman's knees. "I'd be proud."

Mrs. Carr blinked hard, then covered up her emotion by saying, "Jeffrey wants to take you to the Christmas ball. We'll need to get a dress made for you."

"Another dress?" Cherish looked astonished. "But this one is so pretty!" She caressed the folds of the dark blue merino she wore.

"Gracious, Cherish, you can't wear that to a ball!"

"What's a ball, anyway?" Cherish wanted to know.

"It's a big party. They have dancing and games and good things to eat."

"I don't want to dan—" Cherish stopped in the middle of the word.

A glow of pleasure came to Mrs. Carr's face. "Then you shan't." Her eyes took in the girlish figure, the honest eyes. "Jeffrey has his heart set on showing you off. Besides, that Miss Temple may quit pursuing him if he brings another girl, especially as pretty as you."

Cherish felt torn inside. "Would it help Jeffrey if I went?"

"It might. At any rate, you don't have to

dance. We'll arrange for Jeffrey to get you there late, just in time for supper. I wouldn't allow you to go at all except a lot of the hospital folks will be there and you can meet them. Then, too, Felicia will be there."

Cherish heaved a sigh of resignation. "All right. Jeffrey's done so much for me, I can't refuse to help him."

While Mrs. Carr sewed and stitched the beautiful violet silk Jeffrey had managed to procure in some unknown way, Cherish was almost apathetic. What difference did it make what she wore so long as she was clean? But when the gown was finished and Mrs. Carr turned Cherish to inspect herself, she couldn't help feeling a thrill.

The girl in the glass was no child of the mountains.

She was not even the Cherish who had come to Charlotte.

A beautiful stranger stood facing her, although her own violet eyes with tiny brown specks looked back. The violet silk was exactly the same color as those wide eyes. A wide hoop Cherish was sure would trip her held the beautiful material out to best advantage. The modest neckline showed a little of Cherish's white neck, and a locket on a ribbon circled her throat. An overskirt of deeper violet swept back to show off the ruffles finishing the bottom.

"It can't be me!" Cherish gasped. Mrs. Carr had loosened her rippling brown hair from its accustomed coil and swept it high on the back of her head in a simple style all its own. Tiny tendrils escaped to frame the face paling and flushing by turns.

"I'd say it turned out right nice." Mrs. Carr beamed.

"I'd say the same thing." Jeffrey's husky voice came from the doorway. Tall, straight, wearing the finest brocaded vest, cravat, and frock coat, he stepped straight to Cherish and held out his arm. "M'lady."

"I wonder what Dr. Luke'd think of me now?"

The innocent question intercepted looks between Jeffrey Carr and his mother. For a moment the sight of Cherish had bowled over Jeffrey. Now he reassured, "He would think you are beautiful — but no more so than in your little blue frock."

Gladness made her even more lovely. "If I have to go meet a bunch of strangers, I guess I might as well go looking pretty." Her unself-conscious evaluation brought a smile to Jeffrey's lips that lingered long after they reached the ball.

It faded as they stepped inside. The first

163

person to greet them was Felicia. "About time!" She slipped a too-familiar arm under Jeffrey's. "Why —" the white shoulders framed in bright red froze "— who on earth —"

"I believe you have met Miss Hathaway. Come, Cherish, I believe we are just in time for dinner." With an urbane smile Jeffrey led her away, leaving Felicia standing with mouth slightly open.

"I think she was surprised." Cherish could feel mischief coming on. Was it the effect of the dress, the strange image she had seen in the mirror? Whenever she caught sight of herself reflected in the many lamps her confidence rose. Scores of people pressed forward to meet her. Dozens of young men claimed the privilege of dancing with her after supper. She only shook her head. "I don't dance." When they pressed her, she told them in her frank way, "It doesn't seem nice — putting your arms around someone who isn't betrothed to you." Wonder of wonders, they accepted it, simply because of her openness and loveliness.

"Where'd you find her, Dr. Carr?"

"Yes, where *did* you find her?" Felicia appeared at his elbow, eyes hard. "She isn't the same chit I saw in that old blue dress, is she?"

"Her name is Miss Hathaway. That's all that need concern you." He must warn Cherish before it was too late to keep silent about her heritage. Felicia Temple would have a field day with the truth.

He was thirty seconds too late. Before he could quite get to her he heard her clear voice, "Why, I lived in Stump Holler. When Dr. Luke came —"

"Dr. Luke!" Felicia's shocked voice attracted attention from everyone near. "You don't mean Edward Lucas, do you?"

Cherish was instantly alerted. Too late she remembered the look of misery on Jeffrey's face that day so long ago, the bitterness of Dr. Luke when she first met him. Had she done something terrible in mentioning him? The crowd had grown curiously still.

Felicia repeated sharply, "Do you know Edward Lucas? Answer me!"

From somewhere inside came the presence of peace Cherish carried as a constant reminder of her Lord. It strengthened her, gave her a natural dignity as she replied, "Those he takes care of just call him Dr. Luke."

"But, my dear!" a nearby woman protested, hands fluttering. "You can't mean Edward Lucas is practicing in some remote mountain area. Why, before the trial he —"

Cherish lost the rest of the statement in the look of triumph Felicia gave her. What had she done? If only the earth would open and snatch her away from this staring crowd.

Felicia took the stage again as soon as possible. "Well, is Edward Lucas practicing in your — Stump Hollow, wasn't it?"

Green eyes clashed with violet as Cherish quietly surveyed the woman in red then said just as quietly, "Dr. Luke takes care of folks who'll let him."

Felicia pounced on the words. "Those who'll *let* him! What's that supposed to mean?"

Cherish had never been more miserable. The next moment Jeffrey's strong fingers bit into her arm as he led her away saying, "Come, Cherish. We're seated at the head table."

Cherish fought tears and won, although her heart ached. Her inner prayer for strength had been answered. She even smiled tremulously at Jeffrey when he asked, "Are you all right?"

With all her heart she wanted to shout, "No! I should never have come here. Folks in Stump Holler are cruel because of ignorance. Folks here choose to be so." A wave of homesickness threatened to sweep her onto its treacherous reefs. If only she could go home! Not to Mother Carr, although she loved her. Not to Jed, there never had been a home there. But to Uncle Billy and the mountains.

And to Dr. Luke.

Her face went deathly pale. She clutched at the table's edge for support. So that was it — when she'd heard the scorn in that scarlet woman's voice she had wanted to lash out in Dr. Luke's defense, to tell them all how kind and good he was.

I love him.

The words shouted themselves in her heart, washing away her pallor, flooding her face with color. A surge of joy filled her, erasing the trouble from her heart. She reviewed their meetings, all the time responding with mechanical nods and smiles to Jeffrey and the others who attempted to draw her into conversation. When had the feeling started? When she kissed him? When she cared for him and took out the bullet? Or when she first saw him by the old still and instinctively threw him aside from the path of Jed's bullet?

No, there was no moment she could pin down. Love had not been lightning in the sky. Love had come as she learned to know and respect him for the man he was, the man God called him to be.

Hard on the thought came the inevitable question, Could he ever care for her? She was only a mountain girl. He belonged to this world, where she could never enter. She looked around the long tables. Were she and Jeffrey the only ones there not lifting their glasses? She had thought hers contained water, and eagerly raised it to her lips to be stopped by the odor.

A flash of insight caused her to look from face to face. Were these well-dressed people who drank freely and held glasses for more really any different from Jed and his cronies? Suddenly she felt ill. "Could we go? We don't belong here."

Jeffrey was on his feet instantly. "Certainly." He turned to the doctor beside him. "Miss Hathaway isn't feeling well. Please make our apologies to our hosts."

"Of course. Anything I can do to help?" but Jeffrey had already hurried Cherish out a small door in back of the tables. Silently he helped her to the carriage and carefully tucked in her hoop skirt, then gave the driver a low order.

"It's my fault. I never should have taken you to the ball." Jeffrey paused. "I didn't believe even Felicia Temple could be so

168

rude." He turned to face her. "I don't blame you for being upset."

"She didn't bother me so much." Cherish faltered. "It was the drinkin' — it reminded me of Jed. Why would they all look down on him and yet do the same thing? Won't God consider they are all the same? And Miss Temple. Is she any better than the girl in Stump Holler they all talked about because she ran after the men? She wears dresses that almost fall off her. She knows what it will do to men. Then isn't she guilty in God's eyes?"

Jeffrey could not answer. Through the clear eyes of this mountain girl his own understanding became clearer.

"I want to go home. I don't belong here! Your mother knows my God, but somehow He seems lost down here."

What he said would be vitally important. Jeffrey took both cold hands in his. She had forgotten her gloves in their hasty exit. "Cherish, didn't you say God would be here as well as in the mountains?"

Cherish couldn't hold back a cry. "But if He were there tonight He must have been crying! It was a Christmas ball. It was decorated and furnished fine. I looked for somethin' to show it was the celebration of the Lord Jesus' birthday. There wasn't anything. Jeffrey, even the worst folks in Stump Holler take time off at Christmas to think about whose day it is."

"I know. But you came here to learn to help people. You start in a few weeks — the doctors have agreed to let you begin right after the holidays. If you work hard you can be back in Stump Hollow by next Christmas. Are you going to throw it all away, Cherish? What will Dr. Luke think if you go home now?"

Cherish buried her face in her hands. He was right. She couldn't let Dr. Luke down, not now after realizing every beat of her heart carried love for him. She must stay and learn. Someday she might even be worthy — if he loved her. But it wasn't just for Dr. Luke. God had been so good to her, bringing her away from Jed, letting her walk straight after so long. How could she refuse training that would help her take care of other folks the same way the nurses had cared for her?

Yet not even Jeffrey could more than dimly suspect what it cost her to whisper, "I'll stay."

10

Cherish took to training and her studies as a bird takes to flying. She worked and studied as cold weather gave way to spring. She worked and studied as the dogwood and redbud swelled, then blossomed. She continued while the laurel came and went and through the long, sweltering days of summer. When the heat threatened to undo her good intentions, she thought of the cooling breezes on the mountaintop and found strength to go on.

Mrs. Carr fretted. Jeffrey stormed. She listened, then went on with her self-imposed task of becoming the best. Time enough to rest later. She must learn! In spite of her studies there were gaps in her background, and she must fill them.

The hospital personnel respected her. The patients loved her. No patient was ever too fractious for her; she had patience unlimited. One evening Jeffrey paid a visit to the big room Cherish had once occupied as a patient. It was in perfect order.

Cherish was with a dying man behind a curtain. Jeffrey stood transfixed at what was happening. The big man's hoarse voice reached him. "Nurse, I'm afraid to die!"

Cherish's low voice had the clearness of a bell. "There's no need to be. Unless —"

"Yes?"

Jeffrey could picture the patient leaning forward.

"Unless you don't know the Lord Jesus Christ. That makes all the difference."

"My mother knew Him." Was it shame in the husky voice?

"That isn't good enough. God sent His only Son so if we believe on Him we could have everlasting life. He made heaven more beautiful than we could imagine — but we have to confess ourselves as sinners and claim salvation through Jesus."

"But I've done awful things! He couldn't forgive me!"

"Jesus didn't come to save the righteous." Jeffrey's eyes were wet as the steady voice continued. "He came to save sinners. We are all sinners, but the greatest sin is not believing on and accepting Him, and seeing we are sinners."

"If I only had time —"

"It only takes a minute to tell God we're

sorry and ask Him to save us through His Son, Jesus."

Jeffrey slipped away, heart bursting. Later he made a more official visit. The man was dead, but the peace on his face was worth seeing.

Another time he found her seated in a big rocker, singing a small patient to sleep, while the others around strained their ears to hear her voice.

"Do you charm them?" Jeffrey asked her.

"We always sang young'ns to sleep back home." The wistfulness she always felt when thinking of Stump Hollow filled her throat. "I don't think they are any different here. They miss their mothers' arms and good-night kisses."

Strangely enough, no one was jealous of Cherish. She was always there to take on extra work and lend a helping hand. Her own simplicity kept her from offending. In spite of missing Dr. Luke and Uncle Billy and Sam and his family, she was content. Her time would be up in a few months and she would take back with her something of value to the mountain people, even if she had to fight Widder Black.

A few letters had come from Dr. Luke. He said he was so busy there wasn't much time to write, even when there was someone going as far as Singing Waters to mail letters. She answered, pouring out on papers the things she was learning.

In one letter she said, "I can't believe how much folks here need their souls mended, almost as much as their bodies. God seems to get left out. I went to a big church the other day. The music was beautiful, but I'd rather hear Uncle Billy talk. He's easier to understand."

Another time she wrote, "Jeffrey and Mother Carr are wonderful. I will hate leaving them."

Then, "The doctors here have asked me to stay at the hospital after I finish my studies. I know it's an honor."

If she could have known how Dr. Luke would feel when reading what she had written, Cherish would have thrown down her pen. She sensed his discouragement even in his rare communications, but had no way to know the battle he was having with Widder Black. For every victory there was a defeat. The day he got Cherish's letter he had just come from the bedside of a child. He had been called, but too late. A miscalculation in the amount of "yarbs" had killed the little girl. Widder Black was sanctimoniously telling the parents " 'twas the will o' God." Dr. Luke compressed his lips and clenched his hands until the fingernails bit into his palms to keep from bodily throwing the old hypocrite out.

He didn't answer Cherish's letter. She waited and waited and got no word from him. Had he decided it was best for her to stay in Charlotte and didn't want to say so? Had he somehow discovered she cared — a hot flush rolled over her throat and face — and couldn't tell her he had no feeling in return?

Summer droned on. Early fall came, and with it an unexpected visitor to the Carr cottage. Jeffrey had taken his mother on an errand, leaving Cherish home alone, too tired and discouraged to go. It had been weeks since she had heard from Dr. Luke. She had received a short scrawl from Uncle Billy the week before. He hadn't said anything about Dr. Luke except he was busy, so she knew Dr. Luke wasn't ill. Uncle Billy was "feelin' a powerful lot better" and "lookin' fer when Cherish'd git home." She had laughed and cried over the letter.

A knock on the door roused Cherish from her half-daydream after she'd fallen onto her little white bed. She dispiritedly ran her hands over her hair before answering.

Felicia Temple stood on the porch.

Cherish was so startled she couldn't speak.

"Well, may I come in?" There was no friendliness in the woman's demand.

Cherish found her voice. "Jeffrey, Mrs. Carr — they aren't home."

"I didn't come to see them. I came to see you." Something in her animosity set Cherish on guard even as she stepped aside for the wide hoops of the pumpkin-colored gown to enter.

Cherish silently motioned the woman to a chair, hoping she would not stay long. Jeffrey's warning of long ago to have nothing to do with the woman plus her own feelings the night of the ball merged into waiting to see why she had come.

"You need't sit there so demure," Felicia sneered, her usually well-groomed face contorted with ugliness. "I made it my business to find out about you. Do all your friends at the hospital know you were bought and paid for by Dr. Edward Lucas?" Her laugh grated on Cherish's nerves. "Dr. Luke, the pure! Shall I tell you about him?" Never had Cherish heard such an evil laugh. "We were engaged. He was to be head of the hospital here. Then one night he ran down an old man."

Cherish listened in growing horror. Bits and pieces from the past began to fall into place: Dr. Luke's delirious mutterings; the look on Jeffrey's face. She opened her mouth to defend Dr. Luke, but stopped. If Jeffrey and Dr. Luke were still friends, whatever lay between them was not to be discussed with this woman.

"At the trial they proved the old man was already dead before the carriage struck him. But they didn't show why Dr. Edward Lucas was so anxious to run away and leave the old man in the street." Felicia's satin-smooth forehead wrinkled. "I've never figured that out, either — but I will." Her promise chilled Cherish.

"If you don't believe me, about the engagement, you can ask Jeffrey," Felicia preened. "He was in love with me, too. Now he has some quixotic idea about staying away from me because of Edward."

Cherish couldn't have spoken if her life depended on it.

Her silence seemed to inflame Felicia. "I suppose you're sitting there wondering why I broke the engagement. I didn't. Someday Edward Lucas will come back, and I'll be here waiting."

She's lying. There is a flicker in those green eyes. The thought gave her strength enough to stand and say, "Please, would you go now?" She gripped the edge of a table to keep from falling.

Felicia rose to full height. Her glare would have shriveled anyone less protected than Cherish, who had received a great rush of peace from the silent prayer her heart offered. "You dare order me out?"

For a moment Cherish thought the beautifully manicured hand would strike her.

"Shall I tell you more about your precious 'Dr. Luke'? Men don't buy girls unless they expect to get more than their invest—"

"Please!" Cherish stretched out both hands imploringly. "Don't say such terrible things. They aren't true. Dr. Luke bought me so I could be free."

"That's not the way I heard it." The cruel voice sent whiplash stings to Cherish's sensitive spirit. "I sent a man to Stump Hollow." She ignored Cherish's gasp. "He talked with your father. He talked with others who said Dr. Luke cast a spell on your father and got you. He even saw the shack where Dr. Luke lives. You don't honestly think Edward Lucas will stay there, do you?"

Cherish moistened her lips. "If it's what God wants him to do."

Mockery rang out in Felicia's laugh. "You are really an idiot! I don't see how he's stood it there until now. He'll be back." She shrugged her shoulders self-confidently. "When he does, I'll be here."

Her eyes became twin green stones. "As for you, I came here to do my duty and tell you if you have any idea of Dr. Luke, as you call him, ever caring for you —" She stepped closer to Cherish, hands clenching. "We have a name for such as you here in Charlotte." She spat out an ugly word, one Cherish knew only too well from Jed's drunken sprees.

"Get out, Felicia." A controlled voice came from the doorway. Cherish collapsed into a chair in relief. "Oh, Jeffrey, I'm glad you're here!"

"Get out, Felicia," he repeated, eyes deadly. "And if ever I hear of your coming here again or doing anything to harm this innocent girl I swear I'll —" He raised his arm as if to strike down the serpent she seemed at that moment.

"Jeffrey, no!" Cherish sprang to him and caught his arm.

Slowly the look of hatred in Jeffrey's face gave way to contempt so great even the proud Felicia could not help seeing it. "You can give thanks to whatever gods you believe in, if any, that Cherish was here to stop me, Felicia." He swung the door open, letting in a blast of humid air.

Cowed for perhaps the first time in her life, Felicia slunk away to her carriage.

Cherish covered her face. One dry sob tore from her throat. "She called me — how could she —"

"She is everything she would like to believe you are."

Cherish was appalled at his bitterness.

"I told you someday I'd tell you how evil she is." He broke off as footsteps approached. Surely Felicia wouldn't return after what had happened!

It was not Felicia, but Mrs. Carr. "Wasn't that Miss Temple just leaving? What did she want?" She cast a worried glance toward Jeffrey, then Cherish.

"To make trouble, as usual." Jeffrey measured his mother in a probing look and set his jaw. "Mother, you're a lot better these past few months, aren't you?"

"Certainly." She seated herself on the couch. "Cherish is better medicine than all you prescribe!" She made a face at her son.

"Then it's time for a long-overdue story to be told."

Mrs. Carr leaned forward intently, pressing her lips together but making no other sign.

180

Cherish held her breath. Now she would discover those last pieces to the puzzle of Jeffrey and Felicia — and Dr. Luke.

"The day Cherish came you said we were happier when we struggled," he told his mother. "You were right. When money began coming in I guess it went to my head. I began to long to be in the social set, really one of them. Dr. Luke tried to make me see it wasn't worth the price I'd pay. I laughed at him. I drank and rode, raced in the streets and gambled until the hospital warned me that one more piece of publicity would be the end for me with them." He quickly sketched in what had happened and finished with, "I'd brought you here by then and couldn't take the chance of letting you know, Mother."

"You should have told me, Jeffrey!" Her eyes were bright with unshed tears.

"I would have done it long ago," Jeffrey said hoarsely, "but I was afraid your heart couldn't stand it."

"The good Lord'll give my heart strength enough to stand what it must." There was a touch of asperity in her voice. "When He's ready for me, He'll take me. Now," — her keen eyes fixed on her son — "what are you going to do about it?"

Never had Cherish seen Jeffrey so magnificent. Compassion filled her as he quietly replied, "I am going to tell the truth." He started for the door.

"Son," Mrs. Carr quoted, " 'all things work together for good to them that love God.' If Dr. Luke hadn't gone to Stump Hollow, Cherish wouldn't be able to walk straight. And Dr. Luke wouldn't have found out how much the Lord Jesus Christ means in his life."

A glitter in Jeffrey's eyes was the only sign he understood. "It doesn't excuse the abominable thing I did when I robbed him of everything he loved."

A little chill ran down Cherish's spine. Surely he couldn't mean — yet hadn't Felicia said Dr. Luke had been engaged to her? Suddenly she had to know. "Were you — was Dr. Luke — Felicia —" She couldn't go on.

"Guilty as charged." Jeffrey's lips knotted. "He saw her for what she was the night I confessed what I'd done. It took me longer."

"Then she didn't break the engagement?" The room waited for Jeffrey's reassurance, the very air seemed to stand motionless.

"Hardly." Jeffrey's laugh was short. "He was always too big for her."

"She said if he came back she'd be waiting."

"She'll wait a long time before Edward Lucas shows up on her doorstep." Jeffrey stared at Cherish. "He's interested elsewhere."

There was no mistaking his meaning. Cherish put her hands over her burning face to cover the betraying red.

"Don't be ashamed of loving him, Cherish." Jeffrey's eyes were sad but kind. "Any man would be proud to have a woman like you care for him." He bowed and stepped out the door, leaving Cherish alone with Mrs. Carr.

"He's right, you know," Mrs. Carr stood and crossed to the alcove off the kitchen. "I know of no man on earth, including my own son, who wouldn't give all he owns to be loved by you." Her motherly smile warmed Cherish, driving away a bit of the chill that had settled in her heart from Felicia's words. "Now don't you fret about what that Jezebel said." She patted Cherish's hand and disappeared through the door.

Like a gigantic weight the ugly word Felicia had used settled over Cherish. Would she ever forget it? Were the folks in Stump Hollow whispering the same thing?

What if Dr. Luke heard it? For a terrifying moment her heart seemed to stop from pain. Perhaps he had heard it — that ugly meaning put on his generous deed.

Perhaps that was why he no longer wrote.

Unable to stand the confinement of the formerly loved room, Cherish fled out the door, down the lane, to a big tree in a nearby field. Hours later Jeffrey found her there, crouched on the ground, strangely apathetic about the results of his confession to the hospital directors. He led her home like a child and turned her over to the ministering love of his mother, who fed her warm milk and tucked her in.

But as Jeffrey filled page after page with writing, the mocking face of Felicia Temple floated above him — and he hated her for what she had done to him, Dr. Luke, and most of all — to Cherish.

PART III

11

Dr. Luke put down the pages covered with Jeffrey's writing and stared unseeing through his cabin door. Faint touches of autumn were already yellowing leaves, leaving tinges of red on the vine maple. Summer was gone. Autumn was close, and on its heels was winter.

How much he had changed! If Jeffrey's bold scrawl with news that Charlotte hospital wanted him back as chief surgeon had come even a few months before, he would have sung praises. Now he listlessly pushed aside the pages with the toe of his boot and stepped outside.

The Great Smokies. He didn't believe in spells, but if he did, he would wonder when they first cast their shadow over him. When had his self-imposed exile started changing to a feeling of home — in spite of himself? Was it the shy acceptance of his medical skill by more of the Stump Hollow folk? Even the rumblings from the Widder Black and Jed Hathaway weren't keeping the mountain people away. If only they would come to him first, instead of as a last resort? Too often he followed on the heels of the Widder Black. And most of those times he was either too late or had to fight almost impossible odds to save his patients.

"I love them, Lord." In the long hours on Beautiful's back or alone in his cabin, Dr. Luke had learned to talk aloud to God as he would with a friend. "In spite of their superstition and backwoods ways, I've met men and women here who know more about You and Your Son than I ever dreamed." His lips curved upward. "It isn't always easy, either. Most of them read even more laboriously than Uncle Billy."

The smile faded. A dream that had begun to grow filled his mind. When winter settled in and crops could not be tended, he wanted to promote a school for the older people. Many could barely read, and wrote less. Would Cherish be back to help him?

A quick thrust of pain shot through him. Cherish had evidently grown to love the city. Perhaps she wouldn't be back.

Unable to stand his thoughts longer, he headed down the well-worn path to Uncle Billy's. The old man never failed to give him something of value. Not answers, but principles, based on a lifetime of hardship borne through his faith.

Today was no different. Uncle Billy made no offer to ask what was wrong, although Dr. Luke could see the keen old eyes spotted something the minute he walked in the door.

"Set a spell."

"I'm glad to." Dr. Luke dropped wearily into a chair. "If we get one more case of whooping cough I'll have to send you to take care of it!"

"Have had quite a rash." Uncle Billy's gaze turned toward the window. "Not long now till Cherish comes back. She'll help you."

"I don't know, Uncle Billy." Dr. Luke forced himself to sound calm. "Last I heard they wanted her to stay in Charlotte. Offered her a good nursing job right at the hospital."

"She won't stay."

Dr. Luke's heart pounded at the assurance in Uncle Billy's voice. "She might. She told me a long time ago when she went over the hogback she wasn't going to be like the prodigal son. She said she'd go and never come back."

"Jest talk. She might even wanta stay away. She won't."

"How can you be so sure?"

The old face crinkled into smiles. "Knows she's needed here." Uncle Billy's blue eyes bored into him. "Same way you do."

Dr. Luke didn't answer, and Uncle Billy went on. "It's been botherin' you, ain't it?"

Dr. Luke made a quick decision. "Uncle Billy, when I first came I hated it. I ran away because it saved someone else a lot of misery. I could have been Head Surgeon at the Charlotte hospital and when I gave it up, I was filled with bitterness and hatred. A friend had betrayed me, and —"

"Jeffrey."

Dr. Luke stared. "You know?"

"He told me the whole story afore he went to see you. Didn't know if he'd be welcome."

Dr. Luke's shoulders sagged. "Then you know everything? Even about Felicia? And never let on?"

"Some things aren't fer discussin', leastways till those who've been hurt want to talk." Uncle Billy peered at him. "After all this time you surely ain't regrettin' what you did?"

"No. If I hadn't come here I would have gone on my own way. Now I am trying to go His way." He spread his hands. "Uncle

Billy, it's all over. Jeffrey told the truth. The hospital wants me back."

"An' you want to go." A note of finality saddened the words.

"Yes. No. I don't know." Dr. Luke came to the crux of the matter. "Since I've been here I've felt it was all planned. I believe God allowed everything to happen in Charlotte in order to get me back to Him where I belonged. I've also felt for the past few months that God wants me serving Him right here. But if Cherish stays in the city —"

"Son, I cain't tell you what to do." Uncle Billy reached across the small table between them and significantly patted the bulge in the loose shirt where Dr. Luke carried the Bible Cherish had given him. "But if you truly want answers, you've already got 'em — there."

A wave of love for the mountain man threatened to undo Dr. Luke's composure. He hastily got to his feet. "Thanks for reminding me." His hard hand lay on Uncle Billy's shoulder for a moment. Then he slowly stepped outside. His faithful shadow, Hound, who had forsaken Uncle Billy, trotted along beside him. Dr. Luke scratched behind the dog's ear automatically, but his mind leaped ahead to his cabin and what he intended to do. He had read in the Bible often, but not every day. Now he would search the Scriptures, re-read those that had helped through all the lonely months since Cherish left, wondering what kind of love she had for him.

Dr. Luke's lamp burned late that night. The more he read, the more he felt he was being asked to remain in Stump Hollow. Faces of patients beat against his brain but were dimmed by the magnificent words on the pages he read hungrily, hoarding every word. When he came to Luke 9:62, "And Jesus said unto him, No man having put his hand to the plough and looking back, is fit for the kingdom of God," he quietly closed the Book and blew out his lamp. Heedless of the night air chilling his uncovered hands, he stood in the yard of his log cabin home, watching as the rime turned the world white. Was this how the disciples had felt as Jesus softly said, "Follow Me"? Had Andrew and Peter, Matthew and John experienced this same soul-lifting feeling? Was this why missionaries left homes and families to spend years and sometimes their lives taking the gospel of Jesus Christ to far places?

"It's not just to doctor their bodies," he told the night. "I must also become like

Luke, the great physician, bringing salvation through Christ to their souls."

A great strength filled him. He was one of an army of followers, commissioned to teach and preach! Even the thought of losing Cherish paled before that conviction. God had given him a task to do. He had not promised it would be easy. He had promised strength to do it.

Suddenly aware of how cold it was, Dr. Luke went back into his cabin. Yet he did not have to relight his lamp to find the verse he wanted. It was one he had clung to ever since knowing Cherish was considering staying in Charlotte.

". . . God is faithful, who will not suffer you to be tempted above that ye are able. . . ."

No matter how much he might long to rush to Charlotte and declare his love for Cherish, he would not. She must be free to follow what she felt was God's will in her life just as he had done. She must also be free to choose love that was not just based on gratitude. God would strengthen him to wait. If Cherish was to be part of his life, he would rejoice and give thanks. If not, he would trust God and do what he had to do. Nothing was so important as fulfilling the purpose God had for his life.

He felt as if a great burden had rolled from his shoulders. He prepared for bed and banked the fire against the backlog. Peace touched his soul and he slept, in accord with his God.

The next day he told Uncle Billy, "I'm staying. I believe it's what I am meant to do."

"Good." His friend clasped his hand with a mighty grip. His eyes twinkled. "Found yore answer, did you?"

Dr. Luke's eyes were sober. "It was there all the time. I just hadn't had the courage to look for it."

His elation carried him through the next few weeks. It was nearly Christmas, and Cherish had written wondering if he could come. There would be a little ceremony to finish her training, and it would be nice if he could be there.

The simple invitation created havoc in Dr. Luke's soul. He had made his decision. He had turned his whole life over to God and His will. Was it deliberately walking into temptation to go back? Would it make him dissatisfied, regretful? Yet if he went he could determine Cherish's feelings: gratitude or love, and conviction of where they should work, and if it would be together or separately.

"No!" His vehement reply roused the sleeping Hound. "If my decisions are so wavering, then they aren't worthy of a servant of God. I'll go. I owe her that, even if she never comes back."

As he packed the things he would need, Dr. Luke's mind raced back all those months to his entrance to Stump Hollow. Now the trail would be blurred with snow, the going hard. His jaw tightened. He would make it. He had hardened, too, to meet the challenges of this wild, demanding country.

It seemed an eternity before he reached Asheville, even longer to get to Charlotte. A bad storm slowed progress. By the time they finally reached the Charlotte station it was long past time for the ceremony he'd longed to attend.

Had Cherish searched the audience with her wood-violet eyes, looking for him? He well knew the gray uniform she would be wearing and the white collar, cuffs, and pinafore apron. Yet somehow the image he tried to conjure faded into that of a young woman with curly brown hair in a braid, wearing men's clothing, riding behind him on a mule. For one passionate second he wished he had never mentioned nursing to her.

A wave of shame flooded his face with deep color. Such selfishness had no place in his life. Cherish would be well and strong. He thanked God for it. Yet even as he fought his way to a carriage and was driven to the Carr cottage those early days persisted. Why hadn't he appreciated her more? More important, what would she be like now? It had been nearly a year and a half since she came to Charlotte. He could not expect to find his little friend of the woods.

All his imaginings still did not prepare him for Cherish.

She came to the door, lamp held high, her glowing face alight with laughter at some silly thing Jeffrey had said. He had no way of knowing the violet silk she wore had been packed in a trunk ever since the disastrous ball. She had only put it on to please Mother Carr and Jeffrey in honor of the occasion.

"Cherish?" Dr. Luke felt like a blind man groping toward the light. Where was the curly pigtail, the girlish features? Only the eyes were the same, now enhanced by the color of her dress.

Her fingers nearly dropped the lamp. "Why, Dr. Luke! We didn't think you were coming!"

Even as he murmured, "The train was held up," his heart sank. Unreasonably he wished she had called him "Mister." It would have bridged the chasm that opened between them. Any thought of being tempted to express his feelings and plead with her to return to Stump Hollow died on the spot. She so obviously belonged here. What use would she have of silk dresses in the life he could offer?

"Luke, old man!"

Jeffrey's greeting and outflung arms rescued him. There was no mistaking the joy in his face, and he questioned, "How long can you stay?"

"Until the snow stops and I can get back!" Dr. Luke managed a laugh. Slowly he turned to Cherish. "I'm sorry I couldn't get here earlier."

"She was top of the bunch," Mrs. Carr asserted. For the first time Dr. Luke looked at her. She seemed younger than when he'd met her before. Was it the influence of Cherish in her home?

"She told me she was going to be the best nurse in North Carolina." Jeffrey's grin didn't hide his admiration, and Dr. Luke's heart sank even more.

"That's just what she is. The hospital is going to be lucky to have such a great team. She can assist you when you do your fancy stitching, Luke."

"I'm not going to be here."

His words fell like the breaking of a string of pearls on a mirror.

"Say, old man, you don't mean it!"

It took all Dr. Luke's strength to say, "I mean it. I've thought everything over and feel it's best I stay in Stump Hollow." Unable to read the expression in Cherish's eyes he added, "So if Cherish stays on and uses her training here, I guess it will have to be you she assists."

"Not me." Jeffrey shook his head. "After all that's happened I won't be permitted to keep the head surgeon's post." His face turned humble. "It's all right. The board recognized that in spite of what happened my work has been good. They are allowing me to stay on a year's probation, as a junior surgeon. I'm glad for that much. But I was looking forward to the three of us working together."

Dr. Luke caught Cherish's dismayed look at Jeffrey. "I don't think that would be possible." He tossed aside all pretense. "God has called me to work in Stump Hollow. He has evidently called you two to work here." Obsessed with the idea of not letting Cherish think he expected anything

198

from her he finished with, "Jed's still rampaging on the mountain. It's probably just as well you aren't coming home. There's been a lot of talk."

Why had she gone deadly white? Was she still that afraid of Jed? Dr. Luke managed a light laugh. "That doesn't mean we won't be looking forward to a visit. Uncle Billy's 'jest-a-hankerin' to see his gal.' "

Would no one ever speak? Finally Cherish said, "I see. Well, since the future seems to be settled, maybe we'd better get some rest." She smiled tremulously. "We can talk tomorrow." Without another word she turned and slipped into her room.

Mrs. Carr added her approval. "That's right. Dr. Luke, we could put you up here, but Jeffrey said he wanted you." Her motherly smile warmed his freezing heart. "Good night, boys."

There was no carriage to be had when they stepped into the snowy night. "Hope you don't mind walking," Jeffrey said. "I suppose you get a lot of it up there in the mountains."

"If Beautiful can't get through, I use snowshoes."

By the time they reached the hospital and its nearby quarters Dr. Luke was back in control. The two men stood at the entrance shaking off snow and he said, "Jeffrey, if you don't mind I'd like to just walk through the hospital."

Jeffrey protested. "Wait until tomorrow, and I'll give you the grand tour."

"I'd rather do it alone." A look passed between them, and Jeffrey relented. "Come on to my quarters when you're ready."

"Will there be any trouble about my wandering around?"

Jeffrey shook his head. "I'll arrange it." He stopped a passing gray-gowned nurse, said something in a low tone. She nodded and went on.

"Until later." Jeffrey saluted and turned the other way.

It was one of the strangest experiences Dr. Luke had ever known. He hadn't counted on how half-forgotten memories would rush back to assail him. In this building he had helped save lives. He had stood by the bedsides of others he could not save, hating sickness and disease, longing to learn more and conquer human suffering.

Along with the memories was regret. If only he had been true to his original commitment to Christ! How many times would he have been able to lead others to the

Lord before it was too late? He had learned the true meaning of his "Dr. Luke" nickname through personal loss. He sighed. Wasted years, opportunities lost when he could have ministered to soul as well as body.

Shaking himself back to the present, he continued his long walk down halls that had known countless footsteps of those who served the suffering. He could not relive his past and correct his mistakes. He could only go on and serve as he felt led.

A peep into different rooms showed new equipment. Some made Dr. Luke's eyes glisten. If only he had it in Stump Hollow. Maybe someday he would. Jeffrey might be persuaded to finance at least a few pieces of lifesaving equipment.

He lingered in the hospital, feeling it might be the last time he would be there. Strange, when he stepped back into the fresh air, much of his regret was gone. What counted lay ahead. He had tested and won. Now he was ready to go home.

Jeffrey was still up when Dr. Luke got to his quarters. A certain hardness was in his voice. "All right, let's have it."

Dr. Luke's eyebrows shot up. "Have what?"

"Just why did you so neatly arrange

Cherish's future tonight? You know she came here with the idea of learning and going back."

"So things change." Dr. Luke's answer was short. "She's needed here, isn't she?"

"Of course she is." Jeffrey's eyes were in the shadows.

"Then why question?"

"Don't you want her?"

Dr. Luke spun toward Jeffrey. "By what right do you dare ask me such a thing?"

Jeffrey did not waver. "By the right of a man who loves her more than life itself."

Dr. Luke could feel the blood drain from his face. "I see. Another case like Felicia?" He was sorry the minute he said it.

"That isn't worthy of you, Luke. Felicia is nothing. Cherish is everything."

Dr. Luke held out one hand in repentance. "I know, Jeffrey. It's just that this whole thing is unsettling. I know with all my heart I've made the right decision, but this trip has been like a trip into my past life."

"I know." There was no anger in Jeffrey's words. "You love her, don't you?"

"Second only to my Lord."

"She loves you, Luke. She always has. She only consented to actually come because you wanted her to." His eyes were

202

firm. "I can't stand aside and see you throw away that love."

"I have no choice."

Jeffrey's face took fire. "What is that supposed to mean? She'd follow you to the ends of the earth! Do you think I'm going to let you break her heart on some quixotic gesture?"

Dr. Luke started to speak, but Jeffrey forestalled him. "I'm not through. So maybe you are being called to stay where you are. What makes you think Cherish isn't called to do the same?"

"Only she can know that."

"And you aren't even giving her a chance to find out."

Jeffrey's scorn flayed him. "If she is supposed to come back to Stump Hollow, she'll know. She must not come back because of some feeling of obligation to me or from gratitude. If she ever comes it must not even be just because of her love for me, if what you say is true. Unless I get different 'orders' from God, I will probably spend the rest of my life up there. If she had never known what it was like on the 'Outside' it wouldn't have mattered. Now she does. I can't — she must choose of her own free will."

Jeffrey snorted. "Don't you think you're

carrying your principles a little too far? You don't want me in love with her, but you won't tell her you care. What's she supposed to do? Spend the rest of her life pining away for a lost love?"

"Someday maybe she will care for someone else, even you." Dr. Luke drew in a long, ragged breath. "When it happens, I will be able to rejoice. Don't you see? She must choose without my interference."

Jeffrey shook his head. "I'd like to believe it. But it just won't happen that way. Cherish Hathaway is a one-man woman. Too bad that man happens to be so pigheaded he won't tell her there *is* a choice!"

Every free moment in the next few days when Jeffrey and Dr. Luke were alone Jeffrey hammered at his friend to tell Cherish the truth and offer her a choice. He finally warned, "If you don't tell her, I will."

"You won't do that."

"Won't I? Wait and see."

"If you do, I never want to see you again." Something in his voice silenced Jeffrey for good. He didn't mention it again until the day Dr. Luke was getting ready to leave.

A few minutes before time to go to the depot he strolled in. "Cherish is on duty. I can arrange for you to see her before you go."

At first Dr. Luke thought he would refuse. It might be better just to go without saying good-bye. He inwardly protested. He was no coward to run away.

There was a tiny alcove behind curtains in the hospital area. When Cherish stepped inside, the glow of a candle shone full on her face. She laughed and lighted the lamp on the table. "In the dark, Dr. Luke?"

It was all he could do to stifle the urge to catch her close. Yet if he did, all the patient work of keeping things casual during his visit would be undone. "Just came to say good-bye."

He caught the trembling of her lips, wondering if Jeffrey had been right and she truly cared. It nearly unnerved him.

She held out her hand, still strong but not so brown. "Good-bye, Dr. Luke." For a split second he thought she added under her breath, "Mister." The next moment she added wistfully, "I can never repay you for what you've done for me." She peered into his shadowed face. "I'm beholdin', Dr. Luke."

A moment earlier Dr. Luke had been ready to throw caution away, catch her to him, and declare the love bursting over in his heart. He had even taken an impulsive step toward her. Then her words hit him full force.

Beholdin'.

He was a fool to think there was anything but gratitude there for him. His world shattered into a million tiny pieces. His voice was almost cold. Yet he could not resist pressing anguished lips to the part in her shining brown hair before he fled. Jeffrey had been wrong. So had Uncle Billy. There was nothing left on earth for Dr. Luke except his work — and God.

12

The winter storms beat down on Stump Hollow. Dr. Luke exulted in them. They were no fiercer than the storms inside. Some of his own pain was relieved as he faced howling winds and blowing rain and snow to care for those who called on him. Countless times he forced himself to think of other things than how Cherish could have been helping him, if he had said the word. When he was overwhelmed by memory, he deliberately thought of her in the silk dress. There was no place in Stump Hollow for such finery. Neither was there place in his life for a love based on gratitude.

He was so engrossed he didn't see gathering stormclouds in another area, or if he did, he only laughed. Rumors of Widder Black's and Jed Hathaway's determination to drive him away were just that — rumors. He wouldn't budge. He'd been given work to do and would do it.

Uncle Billy tried to warn him. "Don't go near the Hathaway place. An' be careful how you walk down the trails."

"Just how am I supposed to do that?" Dr. Luke grinned. "Most of my patients are lucky to even have a trail broken to their places."

Uncle Billy shook his head and mumbled something, but Dr. Luke scarcely heard him. There was no time for worrying over two poor souls whose minds were as crooked as their morals. He had enough to do keeping track of all the sick folk on the mountain, for the tide of opinion had swung toward him. Was it because Uncle Billy had announced in church one Sunday that Dr. Luke was staying permanently? Or was it just that the necessary months of people to accept a "flatland furriner" had passed? Whatever the reason, there was never more than a day or two between calls and sometimes several in one day.

Sam Ryan asked one day as he walked Dr. Luke part way home from tending to his "ailing least'n," "Wasn't Cherish s'posed to get back this winter?"

Dr. Luke controlled the betraying bounce of his heart and kept his tone even. "She was offered a fine job at the Charlotte hospital."

For a moment the heavily bearded mountain man rubbed one hand over his face and looked across the gap in the mountains " 'Twon't last long. She's mountain born 'n' bred."

Dr. Luke's treacherous heart jiggled again. "Think so? She wasn't treated so well up here."

Sam flushed at the dry tone in the doctor's voice. "We-all learnt to know her after you come." He sounded defensive. "Did that friend of yores really fix it so she could walk?"

"Yes." An image of Cherish standing straight and proud blurred Dr. Luke's vision.

Sam shook his head sagely. "Reckon when the runoff comes so'll Cherish."

"I wish it would come. I'm getting mighty tired of winter."

"Cheer up, Doc. 'Tain't long till spring."

Sam was right. The snows gradually disappeared. Here and there sprouts of green sprang up. Within a week they multiplied. Spring birds began their songs. Every river, creek, and branch ran high.

One day Jed Hathaway disappeared.

No one thought of it much until the Widder Black announced at the ramshackle store, "Wonder where Jed's gone? Hmmm?" and looked straight at Dr. Luke.

"Who cares?" A lounger cackled. Now

that weather was better a few who were too lazy to start planting crops hung around the store.

"Some folks'd better care." There was a veiled threat in the old woman's eyes. "Don't 'spect anyone'd wanta be tried for murder."

Dr. Luke laughed outright. "Who'd murder Jed Hathaway?"

"I ain't tellin'." She swept from the store, leaving the men staring after her.

It was only the beginning. From that tiny drip of poison, all kinds of wild stories grew. The only breath of truth in any of them was the unmistakable fact of Jed Hathaway's absence. To cap it off, Widder Black walked around as if she'd been left a fortune. Even Dr. Luke felt a trickle of discomfort when meeting the beady black eyes. She was up to something.

"That old hag. How can I stop her spreading her lies?" Dr. Luke pounded the sturdy table in front of him. "She's practically accused me of murdering Jed Hathaway. I haven't even seen the old goat for months — not since I came back from Charlotte."

Uncle Billy's face was serious. "She's gotta be stopped. A few folks'll listen to her an' add to it till —"

Dr. Luke wasn't listening. "Guess I'd better drop everything else and go look for Jed Hathaway."

"I'd better go with you. If he should be dead an' you packed him in, 'twouldn't look good."

"You don't honestly think anyone believes me capable of murder!" Dr. Luke threw wide his hands. "After I've treated half the county?"

"Son, it's like I said when you first come — there's good folks and bad folks and lotsa in between."

When Dr. Luke went back to his cabin he was more depressed than he'd been in months. Wasn't it enough to accept God's will, stay here in Stump Hollow and give up all chance of marrying Cherish? Why should he be subjected to all this misery, being accused of murder!

Yet hadn't Jesus been accused, beaten, spit on? Was he greater than his Master, to be protected and shielded from the evils of the world? Shame filled him. Whatever lay ahead, he was a child of God and under the covering of his heavenly Father. If God allowed terrible things to happen, He would also use them for a greater good — even though Dr. Luke could not see how good could come from this.

One afternoon he walked down to Uncle Billy's. There were three dusty horses tethered to a lilac bush just beginning to swell with purple buds. Cherish! Jeffrey must have brought her! He closed his eyes and swallowed hard, then stepped through the open door.

"Here he is now. Got nothin' to hide."

"Son, these two men gotta talk to you." Was that a warning in Uncle Billy's voice?

The two men stood, burly, dusty, enough alike to be brothers. "Air you Edward Lucas?"

"I am." Feathery strokes along his backbone sent an icy chill.

One of the men pulled back his coat to show a badge. The other drew a paper from a pocket. "Then we gotta take you in."

"Take me in where? And why?" A sinking feeling answered him even before the first man spoke.

"I'm Sheriff Ralston. This here's my deputy, Jones. We got a warrant for yore arrest." The deep voice was solemn. "For the murder of Jed Hathaway."

Jones added, "Got tipped off he'd been kilt. Found his body halfway 'tween here and his place."

Dr. Luke could feel the blood drain from

his face. "But why are you accusing me?"

"Got an eyewitness."

Dr. Luke stared. "That's impossible! I haven't seen Jed Hathaway for months!"

"Prob'ly true," Ralston cackled. "He's been dead fer months."

"Then why hasn't this 'eyewitness' come forward before now? If I'm supposed to have killed Jed, why hasn't this man come and told it until now?"

" 'Tain't no man. It's a woman."

"The Widder Black." Dr. Luke couldn't hold back the words.

The sheriff's eyes gleamed. "Prove's yore guilty. You wouldn't a-known who it was otherwise. Come on!" He snapped handcuffs on Dr. Luke, who was still standing there dazed.

"Hold on. Ain't you even goin' to hear what the boy has to say?" Uncle Billy was blazing mad, white hair standing straight up.

"He kin speak his piece at the trial. Circuit judge'll be at Singin' Waters in a week or two."

"A week or two! I'm going to be jailed for two weeks on this pack of lies?" Dr. Luke jerked back.

"Don't git no ideas about tryin' to git away." Sheriff Ralston's face closed, his chill eyes boring into Dr. Luke. "We got orders to bring you in, and we aim to do it."

"It's all right, son." Uncle Billy shot another glance at Dr. Luke, indicating the pistol in the sheriff's belt. "Go along peaceable. They cain't prove anythin'."

"Don't tell —" Dr. Luke couldn't speak Cherish's name.

Uncle Billy didn't answer, just stood there like an avenging angel as Sheriff Ralston and Jones led Dr. Luke outside.

"Can I at least go back to my cabin for my medical instruments?" Dr. Luke pleaded.

"Nope. You ain't be goin' to need them."

He gave up. Awkwardly he mounted the third horse, having trouble with his manacled hands.

"We'll be right behind you. Don't make no funny moves."

Dr. Luke didn't answer. Bitterness like gall rose inside him. Why was this happening?

Every painful step of the horse from Stump Hollow to Singing Waters jolted Dr. Luke to the very soul. His world was in crumbles. Had he been mistaken in thinking God wanted him to stay in Stump Hollow? Had he sacrificed the position of chief surgeon for nothing? Even in his misery he shook his head. God had not changed, even if circumstances had. The Scriptures he had read that night last fall were still valid.

Suddenly he lifted his head and gulped in great breaths of fresh air. God was with him. He need not fear.

Those moments were a strong foundation for the days ahead. The jail was a single-room shack. The tiny window was so high that even the warming spring sunshine didn't fill it. Dr. Luke tried to read the Bible and found his eyes watering after a few verses. The light was too dim.

It was the first time in years he had had so much time for introspection. Had it really been three years since he rode bitterly out of Charlotte, convinced life was not worth living? Cherish had been gone nearly two years.

The first week was spent in weighing chances for his release. He was innocent. There had been a time long ago when he held murder in his heart for Jed Hathaway, but time had erased it. He would regret Jed's death because of Cherish, but he would not take the blame for it.

The second week was harder. Every day he waited for someone to come visit him

— Uncle Billy, Sam Ryan, or one of the other mountaineers he'd grown to love and respect.

No one came.

Again doubts crept in, to be pushed aside at first, then returning with harder force. Where were they when he needed them? Was he to stand trial alone for a crime he hadn't committed?

Finally the sheriff unlocked the jail door, acting a little reluctant. "Feller brung some clean clothes. You kin wash up in the branch." He patted his pistol significantly. "I'll be watchin' you."

The icy water running swiftly over smooth stones felt wonderful. Dr. Luke scooped great handfuls and poured it over his head, bathing his tired, bloodshot eyes. Clean clothing was even more appreciated.

"Who brought the clothes? Uncle Billy?"

"Nope." Ralston spat tobacco juice against the side of the building. "Some young'n."

Dr. Luke's spirits ebbed to an all-time low. He had been all but forsaken. Only God was with him now. Yet as he shaved with the dull razor the sheriff finally produced, a glow inside began to replace his discouragement. So long as he had God, he was never alone.

"Trial's this afternoon." Sheriff Ralston banged the door shut behind him.

Dr. Luke sank weakly on the hard cot. Today! Suddenly it all seemed rushing at him too fast. For one terrifying moment he sought to hold back time. "God, deliver me from this evil," he prayed. Even as he spoke he heard wagon wheels outside, shouts, and laughter. Tugging his bed a little closer to the wall with the window he clambered on it and peered out, unable to comprehend what he was seeing. The usually sleepy town of Singing Waters had awakened. Wagons, mules, people on foot, streaming down the earthy street.

"Sheriff?"

"Whadda you want?" The burly man was almost directly below the dirty window.

"All those people. Why are they here?"

The sheriff's laugh was unpleasant. "A hangin's somethin' to see. Ain't had one fer quite a spell."

With a final glance at the ever-increasing crowd, Dr. Luke stepped back to the floor. So he was to be the prime attraction for whatever circus might follow. If the sheriff's expectations were to be believed the verdict was guilty before he uttered a word in his own defense. So that was what the pounding had been. A scaffold to hang an innocent man! The only crime he had committed was trying to fit into a world that neither wanted nor tolerated him.

It was too much to grasp. Fortunately, he didn't have long to consider it. A short time later he was herded from the jail toward the general store. Dr. Luke looked curiously around. At least in a crowd this big he would see some of his friends.

There were none.

In the entire crowd of onlookers with expressions ranging from open contempt to mere curiosity, he did not recognize one face. Then a black-clad nemesis sprang from the crowd shouting, "Murderer!"

He recoiled instinctively. He did know one person there: the Widder Black. Accuser, tormentor, her black eyes held a maniacal light of revenge. She would go to any lengths to rid the mountains of him, he knew. It was in her face. Once he was gone, the mountain folk would return to her of necessity and she could continue her witchcraft and killing by overdosing with "yarbs."

Something strummed along his nerves as he stared into the hate-filmed eyes. Yarbs! What if she'd given Jed something that killed him and was covering up by accusing another?

Dr. Luke tore his gaze from hers and desperately scanned the crowd. If only Sam or Uncle Billy would come! What would the hostile crowd do if he shouted aloud the conviction leaping within him? His flare of hope subsided. The crowd did not want to find him innocent. From a laughing group, Widder Black's cry had turned them into a mob. He shivered as they pressed closer and he heard their cries, "String 'im up!" "No-good furriner!"

"Hold on there," Sheriff Ralston ordered. "He gits a fair trial, then we string him up. It's the law."

Dr. Luke could feel warm blood from where he bit his lip to keep from shrieking. Law? Justice? What place had they here?

Then they were inside. The store goods had been shoved aside to make room for the trial. He was led to a chair in front. Behind a table sat a tired-looking judge. His face drooped as if to proclaim one trial more or less wasn't that important. All hope fled. If Dr. Luke had been secretly counting on an impartial judge, that last feeling died in the face of the horse-faced man before him.

"Dr. Edward Lucas. You have been charged with murder. How say you?"

Dr. Luke roused from his near stupor.

219

He opened his mouth to speak. Was this how Jesus felt when He was brought before Pilate?

"How say you?" This time the question was louder.

"Not guilty." Dr. Luke threw his head back, eyes flashing. If he was to be convicted it would not be quietly. "Your honor, I plead not guilty!"

There was a crude roar from the jam-packed store, and it carried out the doors to the others who could not get in.

The judge's gavel came down with surprising force. His hooded eyes glared. "There will be no such outbursts, or I will see every one of you is put out."

It had its effect. The silence was deafening.

The judge turned to the sheriff. "Now suppose you tell us just why this man has been charged with the murder of Jed Hathaway."

Self-importance fairly oozed from Sheriff Ralston. "We got word Jed'd been kilt. Me 'n my deputy rode up to Stump Holler and found him. He'd been dead a long time." The sheriff's face wrinkled. "Wasn't no pretty sight."

"Why wasn't it reported sooner? You say you have an eyewitness?" The judge's questions crackled in the charged atmosphere as if sulphur from a lightning storm still hung in the air.

"We ast the same thing. Widder Black said —"

"Him." Widder Black's bony finger pointed straight at Dr. Luke. "He kotched me after I seen him club poor ol' Jed to death and said if I ever told what I'd seen he'd git me, too!"

"Sit down!"

Dr. Luke hadn't realized her monstrous lie had brought him to his feet, protest in every rigid line of his body.

"You'll get your turn." Those strange eyes pierced him. The judge turned to the old woman. "Suppose you tell us just what you saw."

It was her hour of triumph. Madness outrode everything else in her world. Could no one but he see it? Dr. Luke wondered.

"I was goin' home mindin' my own bizness when I heerd a cry." Her face spit hatred. "It was him. He was beatin' Jed with a stick. I musta made some sound." Her voice dropped. If Dr. Luke hadn't known it was all lies, he would have been hypnotized by her stare into believing the story was true.

She sucked in a fearful breath. "He seed me. He about scairt me to death. Said to keep my mouth shut." She moaned and swayed. "Knew the first time I seen him somethin' awful'd happen. He tried to kill Jed way back then."

"Is that true?" The judge beetled his brows at Dr. Luke.

"I can explain —"

"Answer the question. Did you try to kill Jed Hathaway?"

"No! I knocked him down to shut his dirty mouth."

"About what?"

Dr. Luke closed his lips. He could not bring the name of Cherish into this place.

"I'll tell you why. He was besotted by Jed's daughter!" Widder Black foamed at the mouth. "He even paid money fer her — three hunnert dollars. He witched Jed into signin' a paper —" Her wizened fingers reached into the dusty bag she carried. "Here 'tis."

For one minute Dr. Luke thought the nausea filling him would spill over. The crone must have searched his cabin while he was gone.

"This yours?"

"Yes."

The judge pounded the table again to

control the low thunder. "You bought and paid for a *white* woman?" Righteous indignation filled the no longer bored face. "In the name of all that's holy, what kind of man are you?"

"I —"

The judge shut him off. "You'll get to speak later, but if there's truth in this — this horrible thing you've done, I'll jail you whether you killed Jed or not!"

Bit by bit the damning evidence piled up, plausible, convincing. Dr. Luke could see the judge's lips grow even grimmer. Sheriff Ralston testified, "Minute I told him we had a witness he said right out, 'Widder Black.' Shows he's guilty." The sheriff was enjoying his moment of glory. It shone in every line of his face and ugly smile as he added, "No other way he coulda known."

"He came up here an' started takin' my patients away," the Widder Black shrilled. "Him that kilt a man down in Charlotte."

"Killed a man!" The judge bent his unflinching stare on Dr. Luke. "Any truth in that?"

"I didn't kill anyone. There was an accident. An old man died, but —"

"Tell 'em about the trial, and how you got off by the skin o' yore teeth," shrieked Widder Black. "Hospital wouldn't have him no more. So he come here an' done me outa my work."

Dr. Luke gave up any attempt to answer her charges. "Judge, may I tell my story straight through?"

The judge grunted. "Not now. Getting too late." He fixed his eyes on Sheriff Ralston. "Lock him up until tomorrow."

Hours later Dr. Luke laughed mirthlessly. "This could be my last night on earth, God. I'm not afraid, but there's so much I'm leaving undone. Now I know how you felt when Your friends ran away. I thought I saw Sam Ryan in the crowd when they brought me back, but he turned his head. Ashamed, maybe." He stared through the clean spot he'd rubbed on the dirty windowpane. "At least Cherish has Jeffrey and his mother to take care of her. And You."

He turned from the pitiless stars looking down. Only a miracle could save him, and there was no use thinking about it. Sheer exhaustion claimed him.

Sometime later he thought he heard voices. More curiosity seekers? He snorted in disgust and pulled his jacket over his head to shut out any more sounds. His last waking thought was: *I wish I'd asked Cherish straight out how she felt.*

13

When Dr. Luke awakened, it was with an unexplained sense of peace. His eyes roved the half-clean walls and floor, seeking an explanation. Nothing had changed. Yet as he instinctively reached for the well-worn Bible in his shirt, the peace grew.

Before sunset he might be dead. What of it? God knew he was innocent.

"I only wish I had told Cherish I cared," he whispered. "Was I wrong in wanting her to make her own choice?"

There was no answer but the loud scraping of the sturdy board's being removed from across the outside of the door. "C'mon," Sheriff Ralston's rough growl ordered. "Judge's got no time for wastin'."

Yesterday Dr. Luke had searched the crowd for a friendly face. Today he did not. He kept his eyes on the red-streaked sunrise above town. Was it to be his last? A little smile crossed his face, causing a cessation of the crowd's mumbling. If he died, a far better world awaited him. The Lord

Jesus Christ had paid the price so that he and all others who believed might enter.

It wasn't until he stepped inside the crowded store that he raised his eyes again — and looked straight into the beautiful face of Cherish Hathaway.

For one glad moment he almost cried out. The next, icy control swept through him. Whatever came, her name must not be smirched. Strong fingers bit into his arm, and he whirled. This time there was no need for pretense. "Jeffrey!"

The fiery face of his friend burned into his heart. Jeffrey, here! And — his eyes traveled on — Uncle Billy, breathing heavily, with a triumphant look on his tanned face, although deeply etched lines of weariness warred with the triumph.

Could he keep from crying out in gratitude? They had come, those friends he thought had betrayed him. Cherish had dark circles under her eyes. Her gray nursing gown was smudged as if she had traveled hard. Behind her stood Sam Ryan, his wife, the older children. There were others, men and women who had learned to accept him in spite of their mountain clannishness. Dr. Luke bit his lip. There was a fleeting second when he knew hot tears would fall, but the judge spoke. "Let's get on with this trial."

If anything, his horsey face was even more dour. Yet, bathed in the warmth of his friends' presence, Dr. Luke looked more closely. He saw keen intelligence in the hooded eyes, a firm set to the lips.

"Hang him!" the Widder Black called.

"Silence!" Even she quailed beneath the look in the judge's eye. "You told your story. Now we'll hear what the accused has to say."

Dr. Luke slowly rose to his feet, his mind racing. Could he prove his innocence and still keep out of it how Cherish was involved? In the little pool of silence, a clear voice fell, sending shock ripples through the crowd. "Your Honor, may I speak on behalf of this man?"

"Who are you?" The heavy brows almost met above the judge's nose.

"I am Cherish Hathaway." If she felt the collected gasp from the avid onlookers, she ignored it. Never had Dr. Luke been so proud of her. She was even more glorious than she had been in violet silk. In spite of the little curls escaping from the old-fashioned braid she used to wear and that now crowned her like a queen's coronet, she was poised, at ease, almost smiling at the judge.

"You're the dead man's daughter?" The

judge barely waited for her nod. "Do you believe Edward Lucas killed your father?"

"Never!" she flashed. "He couldn't. There is no man I know who cares more for people, especially the Stump Hollow people." She was magnificent. "When he — Dr. Luke — first came here, he ran across Jed's still through no fault of his own. Jed shot him. I hid and cared for Dr. Luke. I begged him not to tell the law, and he didn't."

"Doesn't that make him even more of a suspect?" the relentless judge probed. Every eye was riveted to her. "Miss Hathaway, did this man buy you?"

"He did." Cherish stood proud and straight. "He wanted Jed to let me go to Charlotte and have my foot straightened. He wanted me to learn how to take care of folks. Jed said no. So Dr. Luke bought me and sent me away."

"Witnesses have said Edward Lucas tried to kill your father earlier."

A red flag waved in Cherish's face. "Jed said terrible things about me." Her voice trembled. "Some folks believed them." She glanced at the Widder Black, who stood open-mouthed nearby. "I know what they say about women who are bought. I swear with God as my witness the only reason

Dr. Luke ever did it was so I could be free. Jed beat me. Once he nearly killed me."

Dr. Luke glanced through the paralyzed crowd. Sympathy had replaced many of the hate-twisted looks of the day before. A few of the women now had tears on their faces.

"The Widder Black claims this doctor was kicked out of his hospital for killing a man."

"That's a lie!" Jeffrey roared and muscled his way to the front. "My carriage hit a man already dead in the street. Dr. Luke was my friend. My mother had a heart condition. I was afraid the shock would kill her. I had accidentally left Dr. Luke's bag when I ran from the accident. He took the blame and came here." He ignored the judge's raised hand, a look of shame crossing his face. "Dr. Luke found people who needed him here. He also found God." The room was still. "Because of it he felt he should stay here, even though the Charlotte hospital begged him to come back."

Big Sam Ryan stood. "He saved my woman and young'n — after *she* said 'twas God's will that they die." He pointed to the Widder Black.

Other voices chimed in. The judge

pounded the table in front of him until it bounced. "Enough!" He bent his stare toward Jeffrey. "Even if all you say is true, it doesn't prove he didn't murder Jed Hathaway."

"Judge —" Uncle Billy had never looked so serious in all the time Dr. Luke had known him "— I reckon if I kin speak my piece it'll save a lot of yore time."

"Go ahead." The judge sourly sat back. "Everyone else has."

Uncle Billy almost seemed to be enjoying himself, Dr. Luke thought. The old man hitched his suspenders a little higher. "After Dr. Carr an' Cherish come, we did some prowlin'." He slowly pulled a stained bag from his pocket. "If Widder Black seen Dr. Luke clubbin' Jed Hathaway to death, how come Jed's pouch was in her cabin? Didn't she say she run when the doc threatened her?"

Dr. Luke's brain could scarcely grasp the full meaning of what Uncle Billy was saying. But there was no misunderstanding the effect that dangling bag had on the Widder Black. Time-blackened hands clutched at dusty bonnet strings, and fear shriveled her face until it was ghastly. As if a great river had swept over debris damming its progress, words poured from her.

"No! 'Twasn't my fault! Jed was sick and come fer somethin'. It didn't help." She licked straining lips. Dr. Luke couldn't watch her anymore. She was no longer an enemy — just a pitiful, bound person, trying to justify herself. "He begged fer more, an' when I give it to him he made a sound and keeled over."

"So you *did* kill him!" Dr. Luke couldn't keep it back.

"It was an accydent, jest like what he said." Widder Black pointed a shaking finger at Jeffrey.

"Dr. Lucas." The judge broke the trance over the room. "Do you want to swear out a warrant for her arrest?"

In a flash Dr. Luke knew it had come, the final battle that had been building since he first came to Stump Hollow. The agony of all the indignities and the false accusation rose within him to call down revenge on the shivering figure. Instead he asked, "You dragged him from your shack?"

"Yes. When folks begun missin' him I sent word to the law."

"You horrible old witch! You should be hanged on that scaffold right outside the door!" Jeffrey shouted, and a loud cry of agreement supported him.

Every tale of mountain justice Dr. Luke ever heard rose to meet him head on. He blanched, remembering how hours earlier the same mob cry had been for him. "No!"

In two strides he crossed to the cowering creature. "Go away. Leave this place and never come back." His eyes burned into her. "If I ever hear of you giving your poisons to anyone else I'll track you down, do you hear?"

She nodded dumbly, clutching her bonnet strings again. Then a crumpled bill fell from her nerveless hand, and she began to back away.

"Stop her, Dr. Luke! She's got the money you paid Jed."

Dr. Luke quietly put one restraining hand across Jeffrey's shoulders. "Let her have what is left of it. She has to live."

Face livid, Widder Black snatched the bill and stuffed it back inside her bonnet. Then, in a burst of unusual energy, she gathered her worn skirts in her hands and tore through the crowd to disappear from sight.

"Court dismissed." Was that the trace of a smile on the grim lips of the judge? Dr. Luke could not be sure. The next moment the dour look was back, and the judge elbowed out the door, followed by the half-disappointed crowd.

"It is a miracle you came," Dr. Luke managed to get out.

"A miracle — or Uncle Billy?" Jeffrey grinned. Why did Cherish shake her head at him, Dr. Luke wondered as Jeffrey went on. "Once we knew the Widder Black was making charges, finding evidence of what really happened wasn't hard. All it took was some nosing around."

Uncle Billy took up the story. "Widder Black sure'd hid it! After Sam Ryan come hotfootin' it to tell us how the trial was goin' we pitched in and dug."

"Let's get started," Jeffrey suggested. "We're about worn out."

The ride should have been joyful for Dr. Luke. He was cleared. The mountains were rid of the Widder. Jeffrey had spoken as if he recognized the bond between God and man. Would he recognize his need for Jesus and forgiveness? Dr. Luke prayed it would happen.

"Wasn't that a high price to pay to let Widder Black go free?"

Dr. Luke nudged his horse closer to Jeffrey's on the winding trail. "It was nothing compared to what Christ gave to save me — and Widder Black — and you." His heart leaped as he let his horse drop back where the trail narrowed and heard

Jeffrey mutter, "I know." If ever a man was close to accepting Jesus, it was Jeffrey. Dr. Luke stared unseeingly down the green corridor they traveled, past Jeffrey, Cherish, Uncle Billy. *God, help him see himself as a sinner and accept forgiveness. Everything would be worth it, even this final humiliation, in which I saw no good.*

It was almost evening when they reached Stump Hollow. Yet when Dr. Luke sprang to help Cherish dismount he took her hand. "Are you too tired to walk?"

"No." The quiet answer didn't hide the color in her face.

"Come back when yore ready, and we'll have a bite," Uncle Billy called and Jeffrey added, "Don't make it too long. I'm starved."

Silence filled with unasked questions lay between them as they climbed the once-overgrown trail to Dr. Luke's cabin. In the little clearing before it, Dr. Luke put a hand on her shoulder. "Cherish —" he could not go on.

"It's good to be back." She revolved, and Dr. Luke's mind revolved with her. Did she see it through new eyes now, the crude log cabin he called home? Did the twilight streaks stir her as lighted lamps in the city surely had? He was suddenly conscious of his own crumpled, unshaved self. There had been no more bathing or shaving today. Did the mountains reach out to her — or close her in?

"How long are you staying?"

It seemed an eternity before she turned to him, a question in her eyes he scarcely dared admit was there. "It depends."

"On what?" He would give her no help.

The sophistication of her training vanished. In its place was the frankness of the mountain people that had first startled him, then had come to be appreciated. "On how long you are going to be here."

Still he couldn't accept it. "You mean you want to work with me as a team and take care of the folks here?"

"I do." Was his own longing coloring the fervency of her reply?

Dr. Luke pointed toward the cabin. "It's all I have to offer." He gently took her shoulders and pointed away from the mountains, down the way that led to what she had once called the Outside. "It offers a great deal more."

"Not to me." The words were muffled.

Straining against every fiber of his being wanting to hold her close he said, "You'll never know what your coming back has meant. Perhaps my life." Goaded by her silence he continued, "You must have come as soon as you heard about the trial. Uncle Billy says you were here in Stump Hollow with him."

Her face was pearly in the dust, her eyes unfathomable. "I got here the day after you were taken to Singing Waters. Jeffrey came later."

"The day after —" he peered at her more closely. "— but you couldn't have known — you mean you came before hearing what had happened?" Suddenly suspicion shook him. "Did Widder Black send you a message your father was missing?"

The shake of her head was almost imperceptible. "No."

"Then why did you come?"

She seemed to gain inches of dignity. "This is my home. These are my people. This is where I belong."

It took Dr. Luke a moment to adjust. "You mean you are *staying?*" He wasn't aware of how his fingers bit into her arms. "Cherish, are you sure?"

"I am sure. At least for now. Someday God may direct me differently." She paused. "He may not always want you in Stump Hollow either."

He couldn't keep hope from his voice. "Cherish, if I go or stay, will it be with you?"

Her violet eyes shone through the dust. "Mister, if you want me —"

"Want you!" All the repressed longing of months crept into his words. "Only the knowledge that God gave me this work to do has kept me from despair. But you — Jeffrey told me what you were doing there in the hospital, leading people to Christ. Even my love and need for you must not interfere with what God has given you to do." He swallowed hard. "And it can't be from gratitude."

Two arms rose to clasp him. Two lips untainted by cheap caresses silenced him, as they had done that day so long ago.

This time Cherish did not break and run. Instead she asked. "Do you still have my Bible?"

Dr. Luke speechlessly freed one hand and reached for it.

"Turn to Ruth one sixteen."

He obeyed.

With blurred vision he began the age-old pledge of love. "Whither thou goest, I will go —" His voice grew husky. He could no longer distinguish the words in the final gleams of daylight.

Cherish had no need for light. Her eyes glowed like twin garnets as she quoted, ". . . and where thou lodgest, I will lodge:

thy people shall be my people, and thy God, my God." Her clear voice broke in a half-laugh, half-sob. "Mister, don't you understand? I love you!"

With an inarticulate cry, Dr. Luke wrapped his arms around her. The precious Bible, the Word of God, was between them — the signpost that had led to salvation through the Lord Jesus Christ.

He felt Cherish's heart beating next to his own, like a river in flood. Peace such as he had never experienced swept through him. Dr. Luke had found land he loved, the field the Lord had given him to till, and the girl in his arms. They were his forever — to love, honor, Cherish.

We hope you have enjoyed this Large Print book. Other Thorndike, Wheeler or Chivers Press Large Print books are available at your library or directly from the publishers.

For more information about current and upcoming titles, please call or write, without obligation, to:

Publisher
Thorndike Press
295 Kennedy Memorial Drive
Waterville, ME   04901
Tel. (800) 223-1244

Or visit our Web site at:
www.gale.com/thorndike
www.gale.com/wheeler

OR

Chivers Large Print
published by BBC Audiobooks Ltd
St James House, The Square
Lower Bristol Road
Bath BA2 3SB
England
Tel. +44(0) 800 136919
email: bbcaudiobooks@bbc.co.uk
www.bbcaudiobooks.co.uk

All our Large Print titles are designed for easy reading, and all our books are made to last.